"I think it's time for a divorce."

Jack blinked at Mia's words, his mouth suddenly dry. The apprehension exploded in his stomach again, darker, uglier. "Us?"

Mia's smile was slight, her eyes unreadable. "Yes, us."

"Why?"

She sighed, her breath fanning his cheek. She smelled like toothpaste.

"Is there…someone else?" he asked. He hadn't thought of it, not really. There wasn't any time in his life for him to find anyone else and it never occurred to him that she would be looking.

"Someone else?" She laughed. "Someone besides my childhood friend who married me as a favor and who I've seen all of five times in the five years we've been married?"

He couldn't read her anger. Did she want more? Then why the divorce?

"I want…I want a real marriage," she said, lifting her chin. "Your mom is gone. She can't hurt my family anymore. And I want a family. A husband who lives with me. Works with me. Builds a life with me. Loves me."

He stiffened, unable to process what she was saying. She wanted a family? Kids?

"And that's never going to happen with you, Jack, is it?"

Dear Reader,

When I was five my parents took us on our first backpacking trip to Montana and Wyoming. We returned several times and some of my first memories are of the Rocky Mountains and Glacier National Park. One of those memories is falling off a horse and hitting my head on a rock. Despite this early brush with equine disaster, I wanted to be a cowgirl. Out West. With braids.

The next year, my parents booked a week at a Dude Ranch. My brother and his friend ate it up. They got to help with the horses, hang out with the cowboys, do cowboy stuff. I got to sit in the lodge and color. I was not happy. My parents were able to get my cousin and I on a little trail ride with a cute cowboy holding the reins. I remember being put on that horse and feeling it twitch under me. I remember how far the ground was from my feet. I remember how big that horse was and how little I was.

I started to cry, got sick and that was the end of the trail rides.

My mother-in-law owns a horse farm and I have since made my peace with those giant animals and even enjoy riding them. But I am no cowgirl. Despite that, I'm totally fascinated. So dreaming up my heroine Mia Alatore was a pleasure. Tough and salty, a crunchy outer shell around a vulnerable, gooey center. What's not to love? My hero Jack was a tougher nut to crack. He's a scientist closed off from his emotions, only able to think of relationships in terms of experiments and hypothesis. Getting these two to their happily ever after took some hard work! But it all pays off in the end. Please drop me a line at www.molly-okeefe.com to tell me what you think. I love to hear from readers.

Molly O'Keefe

His Wife for One Night
Molly O'Keefe

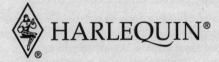

HARLEQUIN®

TORONTO • NEW YORK • LONDON
AMSTERDAM • PARIS • SYDNEY • HAMBURG
STOCKHOLM • ATHENS • TOKYO • MILAN • MADRID
PRAGUE • WARSAW • BUDAPEST • AUCKLAND

Recycling programs
for this product may
not exist in your area.

ISBN-13: 978-0-373-78433-2

HIS WIFE FOR ONE NIGHT

Copyright © 2011 by Molly Fader

www.eHarlequin.com

Printed in U.S.A.

ABOUT THE AUTHOR

This book is as close as Molly O'Keefe is going to get to fulfilling her childhood dream of being a cowgirl, since there are very few cows or horses in downtown Toronto where she lives with her husband and two children.

Books by Molly O'Keefe

HARLEQUIN SUPERROMANCE

1365—FAMILY AT STAKE
1385—HIS BEST FRIEND'S BABY
1392—WHO NEEDS CUPID?
　　　"A Valentine for Rebecca"
1432—UNDERCOVER PROTECTOR
1460—BABY MAKES THREE*
1486—A MAN WORTH KEEPING*
1510—WORTH FIGHTING FOR*
1534—THE SON BETWEEN THEM
1542—THE STORY BETWEEN THEM
1651—THE TEMPTATION OF SAVANNAH O'NEILL**
1657—TYLER O'NEILL'S REDEMPTION**
1663—THE SCANDAL AND CARTER O'NEILL**

*The Mitchells of Riverview Inn
**The Notorious O'Neills

To all the teachers
who engaged and encouraged me.

Especially, Mrs. Jordal,
for not holding that math homework against me.
Mrs. Nelson, who handed me *The Thorn Birds*
and started this whole adventure.
Ms. Mayes,
who taught me it's not good until it's properly
punctuated. Ms. Weidman, who gave the misfits
a place to go and showed me art is equal parts
emotion and intellectual choice.

And Pillen.
Pillen who taught me how to analyze and
improve, hide my nerves, buy a proper jacket,
get over the hard stuff and disappointments
and that the only thing better than hard work
is hard work with chocolate.

Thank you, all of you.

CHAPTER ONE

THE MAPS were…wrong.

Jack McKibbon flipped through the latest topographical charts and compared them to last year's. The permanent compound was being built too far away from the new drill site. His crew would have to take a damn bus between the two. He'd been staring at these maps for an hour and there was no other way to interpret the information.

Someone had screwed up, and considering they were heading back to fix the pump and redrill in El Fasher next month, these kinds of errors could cause serious problems.

He patted through the files, the aerial photos of the well site that needed repair and the embassy report on the recent cease-fire between the Sudanese government and the JEM rebel forces in the Darfur area until he felt the hard edge of his cell phone. The desks in hotels were never big enough.

He flipped open his phone and hit speed dial without even looking.

"Jack?" Oliver, his partner and friend, answered. "Is Mia—"

"Have you looked at the maps?"

"The maps? You brought the maps?" Oliver, a little more jolly than the average hydro-engineer, laughed.

"Of course. I had all the files couriered, they arrived a while ago. I thought you'd want to get a jump on things."

"I can't believe you brought your work to the hotel. One night is not going to make a difference, Jack. How about you take a break. We're going to party. Mia's coming—"

"I'd hardly call it a party," he said, sorting through the mineral reports. He needed to recheck that silver count. That could change the water table information.

"There will be food and booze. By most standards, that actually is a party."

"It's a fundraiser meet and greet," Jack scoffed. Jack was head of research at Cal Poly where Oliver chaired the hydro-engineering department. They'd been working on a lightweight drill and pump that could withstand the extreme desert conditions of Africa and Asia. And over the past four years, these fancy events had become standard operating procedure, before and after every summer, Christmas and spring break spent in the field. But after the success of their drill during last year's sabbatical, Oliver and Jack had brought so much prestige to the school that the administration had decided that more torture, in the form of these cocktail soirees, was in order.

Particularly now, to raise some money for Jack and Oliver's trip next month.

Which would explain why they were here, on the cliffs of Santa Barbara, miles from the university, in an effort to bring up the big bucks from Los Angeles. Africa was a popular charitable cause in Hollywood.

"Just try, Jack."

"Christ, Oliver. The university is trotting us out like trained monkeys—"

"For Mia. Try to get your head out of the dirt for one night."

Right. Mia.

"It's been over a year—"

"I know how long it's been," Jack said. A year and two months, almost to the day.

The excitement of seeing her, when he

remembered, was bright and hot, shooting out sparks.

But these maps…

"When is she supposed to arrive?" Oliver asked and Jack swore, checking his watch.

"Any minute," he said. "I'll see you later."

He hung up and ran a hand over the scruff covering his chin. He'd wanted to be dressed—at least showered—by the time Mia showed up. As if being clean-shaven would somehow make this reunion easier.

But the maps had arrived and he'd gotten distracted.

Jack closed his burning, tired eyes. Jet lag dogged him. Not to mention the malaria he had barely recovered from. He was thirty-five and he felt a hundred and five.

The truth was, he was tired of Africa. Tired of the sand. The heat. The militias. Of coming home sick, only to turn around a few months later to go back. He was tired of never being able to meet the need, of feeling like a failure every time he left. But he couldn't tell Oliver. He couldn't tell anyone.

This had been his dream, water for the thirsty. And to give up on it now felt shameful. Selfish.

And this whole situation with Mia was making his crappy mood worse.

Calling Mia like this…not quite the reunion he'd dreamed about.

I owe you, she'd written in response to his email asking her to come to this event with him.

Owe me, he thought, turning the words over in his mind like a spit of meat over a fire. Logically, that was true.

But there were thirty years of friendship between them. A thousand emails. Promises made and kept.

Mia could be prickly. And his being out of the country for the past year had no doubt made her *very* prickly despite the daily emails.

This reunion of theirs was going to be unpredictable. And not being able to prepare for Mia's mood made him nervous. Was she going to be angry? Happy, like him, just to see each other?

He didn't know and it was making him crazy.

Someone pounded on the door to his hotel suite. The windows rattled as if mortars were being dropped. There was a pause and then more pounding.

It was her. Not that he could tell by the pounding. It was his internal barometer, which measured pressure and changing dynamics better than any equipment he carried into the field.

Warning, that barometer whispered. *Be very, very cautious.*

He ran his hand across the front of his worn T-shirt and crossed the room, his shoes soundless on the broadloom.

He was surprised to feel his heart thudding in his chest. Nerves? he wondered. Excitement?

A month ago he'd stared down a truck full of hostile militiamen and now he stared at the mahogany door, anxious about what stood on the other side.

It wasn't the same kind of anxiety. Mia wouldn't have weapons. He hoped. But she'd be armed with something far trickier and more insidious. Something he couldn't negotiate with and had never known how to handle.

His past.

He opened the door and as expected, it was her.

Mia Alatore.

And his heart slipped the reins of his brain and he was so damn glad to see her. To have her here. Selfishly, she just made him feel good. The world fell away, the maps disappeared, and his whole existence was Mia.

"Good God, Jack, I thought I was going to drive right into the ocean before I found this place. You didn't tell me we'd be hanging over a cliff."

A whole lot of attitude in a tiny package.

She barely came up to his shoulder. Her too-big plaid shirt hung loose on her body. A ball cap, beat-up and white with dried sweat, sat low on her head, keeping her eyes shaded.

She was the same. Exactly the same and part of him rejoiced. In a world gone crazy, Mia Alatore was the same.

Her voice—laced with the sweet accent of her Hispanic heritage—was like a shot of whiskey right to his gut. He'd been to a lot of places, seen sex acts and rituals that would make a monk give up his robes. But nothing in the world was as sexy as Mia's voice.

"I'll keep you out of the ocean, Mia," he said with a smile. Her head jerked up and he got a good look at her wide amber eyes.

There she had changed. Over the past five years, he'd seen her three times, not counting right now, and each time he saw her, her eyes had faded a little more. The fire and glitter worn soft over the years.

He could see the years in those eyes, the darkness where there had only been light.

"Did you have trouble?" he asked, leaning in to carefully kiss her warm, smooth cheek. She smelled like sunshine and horses.

Oddly enough, two of his favorite smells. He could have stood there, sniffing her cheek all day.

"No," she murmured, ducking away and clearing her throat. "But they wouldn't valet my truck. Some punk kid in a uniform made me park in the employee lot."

"I'm surprised they didn't make you park it in the ocean."

"Watch it, Jack," she said with a smile and his chest swelled with fondness. "She'll hear you and she doesn't like water any more than I do."

"It's good to see you," he said, awkwardly patting her shoulder. "Thank you for coming."

"Well," she muttered, "like I said, I figure I owe you." She stepped inside their room. Suite, actually—he made sure she had her own room off the living room. He didn't want there to be any more awkwardness than necessary.

"Nice place," she said, looking around. "Better than the last dump. Being Indiana Jones must pay better than it did a year ago."

Christmas, a year ago, he'd asked her to come to Los Angeles, to sign some legal paperwork before he took his sabbatical. He'd paid little attention to the motel where they'd stayed, not realizing how crappy it was until she pointed it out.

"The university is paying for this. It's part of the…thing."

"The thing?" Her smile was brief but breathtaking, a lightning strike over the Sahara Desert. "You live some kind of life, Jack McKibbon, if people throwing millions of dollars at you is considered just a thing." Her eyes were warm. Fond. He wondered for a minute if she was…proud of him?

How novel.

"It's not at me, per se, it's the university. I mean, it's our research. Our pump. But the money is going to the university. For more research." He was babbling, awkwardly talking about his work, which did not bode well for the night ahead. Another reason he hated these events.

If people wanted to talk science, he could do that all day. But explaining the complex nature of water tables and the ever-changing political nature of Sudan in laymen's terms was impossible for him.

Oliver was better at that stuff.

"Either way. It's a good thing you do." Her smile reached her eyes, crinkling the corners. "Water for the thirsty. Like you always dreamed."

He felt her measuring him, testing him through the years and choices that separated them. Seeing perhaps if she still knew the practical stranger that stood here, found in him the boy she'd known better than anyone else.

He saw that girl he'd known. She was right there in that stubborn line to her chin. The nose that led her into more trouble than one half-size female should ever see.

"I missed you. It's been a long time, Mia," he breathed, the words squeezed through a tight throat.

She blinked, as if jerking herself out of a daze.

"Where do you want me to put my stuff?" she asked, and the moment was shattered. She dropped her duffel on the floor, plumes of dust erupting into the air at the impact.

"There works," he muttered. Whatever was in that bag couldn't be in good shape. "You know, maybe I should have made it clear, but this is a formal thing…"

Her eyes sliced through him. "You worried I'll show up to your fancy shindig with dirt under my nails?"

"No, well, maybe. And I don't care." He reached out his hands, showing her the red dirt that stained the skin around his fingernails. "I just don't want you to be uncomfortable. There's going to be a lot of scrutiny—"

"Because you're Indiana Jones and making Cal Poly a whole bunch of money?" She said it as a joke and guilt clobbered him.

You're an ass, he told himself, *bringing her here to be scrutinized and gossiped about.*

"No," he said and took a deep breath. No other woman in his life owed him enough to stand beside him and face down the firestorm of academia gone wild. "I should have told you this in my email," he said.

"Uh-oh, this doesn't sound good." She crossed her arms over her flannelled chest and those curves she'd always worked so hard to hide were unmistakable.

"Mia, I'm sorry—"

"Out with it, Jack. You always were a wuss when it came to dealing the bad stuff."

That was a low blow and his temper flared. It was easy for her to judge him. She'd stayed. He'd left. Big freaking deal.

"Fine, because the dean has accused me of having an affair with his wife."

She didn't look at him. Not for a long time. The air conditioner kicked on, loud in the silence. He counted her breaths, the rise and fall of her chest, wondering why it mattered.

"Have you?" she asked.

"No, Mia. Of course not. But Beth…the

dean's wife, has been…" How did he put this? "Indiscreet."

"She wants to have an affair with you?"

"So it would seem."

"And you can't just say no?" she asked, her eyes snapping.

"It's delicate," he said.

"You want me to tell her?" she asked. "You made me drive two hundred miles over the mountains two months before calving season, when I'm so busy I can't see straight, to tell some woman to keep her hands off you?"

In a way. In his head it made so much sense. But that was his problem—what worked in his head didn't always translate to other people. To real life.

Mia picked up the duffel bag, leaving dust on the floor. This trip out to Santa Barbara was a big deal for her, he knew that. Things were busy at the Rocky M and as far as he knew, she was still doing most of the work.

And now she was here and angry with him, which wasn't what he wanted at all.

Give him a hundred feet of sand and seventy-mile-an-hour winds, and he could make things work.

Add another person to the equation,

someone he had to deal with face-to-face, and he'd find a way to blow it.

"No, Mia, it's not quite that dramatic. With you here, she won't try anything. And people won't…speculate about an affair. They won't be watching me like a hawk. It will be forgotten."

Her eyes got wide and her lips got tight.

"Because they'll be talking about me," she said. "I'm a distraction?"

He nodded and shrugged. Attempted a smile. "You're my wife."

She nodded once, anger rolling off her like the smell of burned tires. "Sure," she said. "Makes perfect sense. I need to shower."

"Through there," he said, pointing to the far door. "We need to go in a half hour."

MIA SHUT THE DOOR behind her and collapsed against it. The wood cooled her flaming face.

Jack, she thought, gutted. Gutted at the sight of him, the sound of his voice. Hell, the smell of that man killed her. He'd opened that door and her heart beat its way right up into her throat.

I missed you. It's been a long time.

Whose fault is that? she wanted to yell. An emotion she tried so hard to suppress and restrain bubbled up, sticky and insistent.

You left me, she thought. *You married me and left.*

But that had been the deal. She'd known it going in.

This pain was her own damn fault.

If only he weren't so handsome. So familiar and beloved.

The whole drive over the mountains she'd wondered what kind of changes the past year would have carved out of him.

His intelligence still lit up his chocolate eyes like a brilliant pilot light. The crow's-feet growing out of the corners were deeper, from a year spent under a harsh sun. The silver hair peppered through the close-cut blond was a surprise.

His shoulders were broader, the calluses thicker.

Jack was a man who worked. Got his hands dirty and his back bent out of shape. He dug holes and built things and that kind of work made him comfortable in his own skin. Confident in himself.

Which was so different from the angry

and serious kid he'd been. A kid who hadn't known his place in his own family.

But that had all changed. Jack McKibbon knew who he was now and it was so unbelievably sexy.

It was no wonder deans' wives were throwing themselves at him.

The pain cut her off at the knees and she sagged farther down the door.

Maybe tomorrow she'd laugh about it. Or next week. But right now it hurt.

A year and two months since she'd seen him. Since she'd gone to that dive hotel in Los Angeles thinking, like a fool, *Now...now it will change. He's going far away, someplace dangerous, and the fear has made him realize how he feels about me. About us.*

Instead, he'd had her witness his will, sign power of attorney papers. He'd taken her to dinner, thanked her when she gave him the book she got him for Christmas. He slept on his stomach, his face turned to the window in the other bed in their hotel room, while she stared at the ceiling on fire with love and pain.

That should have taught her the lesson she just couldn't seem to learn.

Jack McKibbon didn't love her.

But, once again, she drove over the mountains today, thinking this time was going to be different, too.

It's what she always did. Five years into this nonmarriage and with every email, every phone call, the rare visit, she kept thinking things were going to change.

That he would miss her. That he would wake up in the desert and want her beside him.

You're an idiot, she told herself for perhaps the hundredth time since climbing into her truck a few hours ago.

Her sister Lucy's words rang in her ears. *You've let a crush take over your life. When are you going to let go of the hope this relationship is going to be anything but an afterthought to him?*

Mia'd told herself, over and over again, that if it *was* an afterthought, Jack would end it. And because he didn't end it, hope lived on.

Part of her—a big, stupid part, stupid like dumb, stupid like a fool—believed that he'd invited her here because he wanted to share this moment with her. The realization of all those dreams. Dreams he'd told her about when they were kids in the back of his truck, the desert stretching out around them like the lunar landscape.

Water to the world had been his dream. A pump and drill that could build wells in the deserts of Asia and Africa. She'd been following his progress on the internet. Going into her office at night to cheer him on from her little corner of the thirsty world.

Too many nights doing that. Too many years holding the memory of him close, despite his absence.

Too many years of patiently caring for the ties that bound them together.

Marriage.

His father.

The Rocky M.

Jack had done her a favor five years ago when everyone's lives fell apart. And she was doing him a favor now. It wasn't as if his father could care for himself.

But Mia was kidding herself. She knew that.

Jack McKibbon was never going to see her as a woman. A real wife. Someone to love.

She pressed her head harder into the door,

the pain almost distracting her from the sucking pit of embarrassment and disappointment in her stomach.

It was time for a divorce. She'd do this favor for him tonight. Play the loving wife, face down whatever gossip and scandal the night had in store and then it was time to let him go.

To let the past go.

She had to, because this situation was killing her.

She stood up, the shaking under control. Her emotions in check. No need to get dramatic, she thought. If there was one thing she knew, it was that life always went on. And she could stand here, crying over something that was never hers to begin with, or she could put on her big-girl pants and do what needed to be done.

She glanced at her watch. She had a really wrinkled dress, some makeup, jewelry that looked like torture devices and a whole bunch of instructions from her sister on how to look like a woman rather than a ranch hand.

Tonight she'd be Jack's wife.

Tomorrow she'd work on that divorce.

CHAPTER TWO

JACK SHRUGGED into his suit jacket as he stared down at the aerial shots of the militia compounds surrounding the villages where he and Oliver were digging their wells in Darfur.

The compounds had been built up. More than before, despite the cease-fire. Going back next month wasn't going to be easy.

As if it was ever easy.

Mustering up enthusiasm was impossible.

"Jack?"

"Hmm?" he said, distracted by the desk full of papers. Christ, if Oliver could just do this meet and greet by himself, at least one of them could get some work done tonight.

"Jack!"

"Mia!" He spun. "Sorry, I got—" Jack had some expectations of how Mia would look, stepping out of her bedroom. And he'd be lying if he said those expectations were high. She was a rancher on a hardscrabble pocket of land two hundred miles from here—and she worked that land hard.

Ranching life didn't leave much time for shopping. Or dress wearing.

So the version of Mia standing in the doorway to her bedroom was both expected and a sharp, shocking surprise.

"Distracted," he finished lamely.

The dress, black and simple, was still wrinkled and didn't fit. Too long at the knee and too tight at the bust. Probably her sister, Lucy's. Mia looked uncomfortable just standing in the high-heeled shoes with the sexy bow on the side; he dreaded thinking of her walking in them.

That's what his head noticed anyway.

His body was busy noticing other things and nearly roaring in approval. Her skin, God, her skin was like caramel. And the rustic gold bangles she wore at her wrists made her look like an Incan princess. Her hair was long and loose, the curls riding her back and he wanted to touch those curls, feel them clinging to his fingers, twining around his hand.

But her body…oh, man.

Growing up, he'd thrown a lot of punches against the mouths of boys who'd been too vocal in their admiration for her young body. And he'd gotten used to not looking at her below the chin, out of respect. Friendship. Because he knew how much her curves bothered her. Embarrassed her.

She didn't seem embarrassed now.

The black dress skimmed her breasts, revealing the pillowy tops, the perfect round contours, the mysterious black valley that divided them. And he knew, as awkward as she might feel in that dress, not a single man would notice.

Because all they would see was her beauty.

"I'm going to have to punch out a lot of guys tonight," he murmured, and she smiled.

"I doubt that." She smoothed the front of the simple dress. "It's wrinkled."

"Putting it in a duffel bag will do that," he said.

"Oh, and suddenly you're Mr. Fashion?" She narrowed her eyes, the years melting away under their teasing. "That's not even your suit, is it?"

"Of course it is," he said, running his hands over the too-big jacket. "I've just lost some weight."

Mia stepped forward and pulled the tie from where he'd stuffed it in his suit jacket. She flipped up the stiff edges of his collar and settled the tie around his neck. He lifted his chin, standing willingly under her ministrations. She'd tied his tie on his prom night with Missy Manning, on his graduations from high school and college. The day they got married.

It was the only time in his life, other than the day of their wedding, that Jack actually felt like a husband.

She was close. So close he could see the freckles across her nose, the small scars along her chin where she'd fallen into the barbed wire when they were kids.

Her lips…

He blinked and looked back up at the ceiling.

What a marriage, he thought. He must be the only husband who'd never had a wedding night.

Sometimes he got the impression that Mia wanted something physical between them. She'd watch him a little too long, her eyes dilating, her breath hitching—principal signs of animal attraction.

But he'd told himself since he was twenty years old and she'd been fifteen that nothing would ever happen between them unless she started it.

And she never had.

"Well," she sighed, patting his tie. "It's a little crooked, but no one will notice."

"It's great, Mia," he said through the tension in his throat. "Thank you."

"We're a fine pair," she said with a twinkle in her eye. "Let's go cause a scandal."

And just like that, this night, this torturous night that he'd been dreading with every fiber of his being, was fun. An adventure.

He offered her his elbow and she slipped her hand, small but so strong, up next to his ribs and then around his arm. He felt the pressure of her fingers, the weight of her palm, through his skin and down into the muscle.

"Let's go," he murmured and opened the door to the night.

They crossed the moonlit path from their cabana suite to the glittering main part of the hotel. A crowded patio surrounded by bougainvillea jutted up over the cliffs over-looking the ocean. She stopped, staring off at the water, the oil drills in the distance, the Channel Islands sitting like fat coins on the horizon.

"The islands are so pretty," she said.

"They call them the North American Galápagos," he said. "Because there are over one hundred and fifty endemic species. Plants alone there are—"

"You don't say, Professor," she said, her voice thick with sarcasm.

"Sorry." He ran a hand over his forehead. "I'm—"

"Nervous?" she asked and he turned to face her. Luminous in the moonlight. If only they could stay out here all night.

"I hate these things," he said.

"You do suck at them."

His laugh cleared the adrenaline churning through his stomach. He sighed, and they stood in silence, staring at the islands. The blinking lights of the oil drills.

"I'm glad you're here," he said, and suddenly Mia pulled her hand away from his elbow, creating distance where he didn't really want any.

"We need to talk," she began. He hung his head.

"Not Dad again, Mia—"

"I think it's time for a divorce."

Jack blinked, his mouth suddenly dry. The apprehension exploded in his stomach again, darker, uglier this time. "Us?"

Her smile was slight, her eyes unreadable. "Yes, us."

"Why?"

She sighed, her breath fanning his cheek. She smelled like toothpaste.

"Is there…someone else?" he asked. He hadn't thought of that, not really. There was no time for him to meet anyone else and it had never occurred to him that Mia might.

"Someone else?" She laughed. "Someone besides my childhood friend who married me as a favor and who I've seen all of five times in the five years we've been married?"

He couldn't read her anger. Did she want more for them? Then why the divorce?

"I want…I want a real marriage," she said, lifting her chin. "Your mom is gone. She can't hurt my family anymore. And I want a family. A husband who lives with me. Works with me. Builds a life with me. Loves me."

He stiffened, unable to process what she was saying. She wanted a family? Kids?

"And that's never going to happen with you, is it?"

"No," he answered. She turned away, staring off at the ocean, her jawline as set in stone as he'd ever seen it. The idea of going back to the ranch was laughable. It would be like volunteering to go to hell. His work was on the other side of the world, his life was far away from where he'd been raised and abused by his parents.

"Why?" he asked, because what she wanted didn't make sense to him. "My parents had a 'real' marriage. I don't know why you'd want that."

"My parents had a real marriage, too, Jack. And they were very happy," she said. "Not every relationship is like your folks'."

He didn't say anything, because frankly, while he understood her hypothesis, he hadn't seen enough proof to support it.

"It was always going to end this way," she said, and he kept his eyes on her profile, wondering where this was coming from. "We knew that. It's not like we were ever going to have…something real."

"You're one of the most real things in my life, Mia."

She closed her eyes, a strange anxiety rolling off her.

"We'll always be friends," she finally said. "Divorce, just like the marriage, won't change that."

"Okay." He had to agree, because he supposed logically, she was right.

And there was no arguing with logic.

"We can get a divorce," he said. "If that's what you want."

"That's what I want," she said, with a definitive nod. Her mood shifted and she was suddenly cheerful. Totally at odds with the loss he felt. "I'll put together the paperwork," she said.

He nodded, numb and off course. He wished he could go back to his work, those charts. Even with the errors, he could read them. They made sense.

"All right, then," she said, pulling him into motion, leading him into the party. "I need a drink."

Mɪᴀ's ʜᴇᴀᴅ ʙᴜᴢᴢᴇᴅ. Her stomach churned. A glass of wine on a belly full of nerves and no food wasn't her greatest idea. But she needed something to ease the worst of the pain.

Divorce.

A million times in the years she'd known him, she'd thought about telling Jack how she felt. Maybe if he knew, things would change. But right now, this moment, was why she never did. Because in her heart of hearts she'd always known Jack McKibbon could never return her feelings. Never.

His wounds were too deep, his brain was too big and his heart was just a bit too cold.

And she was always going to be little Mia Alatore.

She took another sip of her white wine and tried to ignore the whispers that buzzed around her like horseflies.

It wasn't hard to guess who the dean's wife was. Mia would put money on the tall redhead staring at her from the corner of the room with enough malice to cut steel.

But the rest of the women at the party were staring at Jack, who, even in his ill-fitting suit, was the handsomest man there. Tall and broad, rough around the edges, he was so different from the slick men surrounding him. Like a wild animal surrounded by domesticated cats.

She'd bet that most of the women in the room wouldn't mind seeing Indiana Jones without the suit.

Herself included.

Maybe she should try to get that wedding night before it was too late.

She snorted into her wineglass.

"Mia?" A vaguely familiar young woman with bright eyes and a slightly plastic smile stepped in front of her. "I'm Claire, Devon Cormick's wife."

"Hi." Mia shook hands with the woman. That's why she was familiar; they'd met three years ago at her first of these cocktail parties. When she'd actually felt like a wife. When hope had made her excited to be on Jack's arm.

"Devon's going to El Fasher with Oliver and Jack in March to fix the drill."

"Next month?" Mia asked, before she could stop herself.

Claire blinked, the plastic fading from her expression. Replaced by a baffled concern that looked, to Mia's jaded eye, like pity. "You…didn't know?"

Mia took a deep breath. "No. I didn't."

She finished her wine and handed the glass off to a passing waiter and without a second thought, picked up another.

She was going to get drunk, and right now, with the pain lancing her body like a thousand arrows, it seemed like a great idea.

"Mia," Claire said, "I'm not sure what the situation is between you and Jack and I certainly am not going to speculate—"

"Really?" Mia asked, not believing it for a minute. She could feel the speculation from every single person in the room like hot air suffocating her.

Claire stiffened, her eyes shooting out sparks. "No," she said. "I'm not. But Devon and Jack are the only two on the team with wives and…"

Realization sunk in. Claire wanted someone to commiserate with. Someone to hold hands with and pray, to pore over the newspapers and pull apart embassy reports.

I have to do this? she asked herself, bitterness making her feel a million years old. She wanted to find her rusty, beat-up truck in the employee lot and head back to the land she loved and that loved her back. *I have to live all of this again?*

"I'm just so scared for him," Claire breathed, and Mia couldn't mistake the fear in the woman's voice.

A fear she knew too well.

"Stay away from the internet," Mia said, staring into her wineglass, sucked unwillingly into the past. The first trip Jack took to Africa, Mia had been glued to her computer and the unsubstantiated reports had given her ulcers. "Try to stay busy. Focused on something other than your husband."

"That's it?" Claire asked. "No internet and get a hobby?"

Mia nodded, remembering the crushing anxiety all too well and knowing that there was nothing Claire could do to really combat it.

"Unless you can convince him not to go?"

"That didn't work with Jack, did it?" Claire asked softly.

Mia finished the wine in her glass, gulping it down without tasting it—wishing the rest of her body could go as numb as her taste buds. "I didn't bother trying," she said.

She and Claire made difficult small talk—it was all too obvious that Claire wanted to ask about Mia's relationship with Jack. Hash it out, woman to woman.

But that wasn't going to happen.

Finally, Claire made some excuse about needing a bathroom and left.

Thank God, Mia thought, stepping onto the balcony where it was quiet. A cool breeze blew off the ocean and her skin chilled. Her nose went cold and her eyes stung.

Jack was leaving. Again. It had become so common; he didn't even bother to tell her anymore.

"There's my girl," a happy British voice said from behind her and Mia turned to see Jack's partner, Oliver.

Mia wasn't what anyone would call a hugger. But the sight of Oliver, his bright, bald head, his dashing dinner jacket with gold buttons, drove her right over the edge and she pushed herself against his barrel chest.

"Whoa there, Mia," he said, stroking her arms. "Are you okay?"

"You're going back," she said against his chest. "Next month."

"He didn't tell you?" Oliver whispered, and at her silence he swore.

"The government and JEM signed a cease-fire."

"That doesn't comfort me, Oliver."

"We'll be fine, Mia. You know that. We have lots of security—"

"And you don't take risks," she said, finishing the line she'd heard seven times over the past four years. Jack and Oliver had the same script.

She stepped away, already regretting the show of emotion. Wishing she could take it all back.

"Are you okay?" he asked.

"Fine." She flashed him a bright smile. "Great. Just surprised. How are you?" She squeezed his big shoulder, a far more Mia-like greeting.

"Bored to tears," Oliver said. "And wishing I had a wife to liven things up at these parties."

"Well, don't do anything drastic," she said, proud that her voice was light. None of her grief or bitterness leaked out.

But Oliver's piercing eyes saw through her. "You and Jack make quite a pair," he said, sipping at a glass of tonic water. "He's about to bite off every single hand that's here to feed us and you look like you're going to cry or start a fight."

"Jack doesn't like these things," she said with a shrug. "And I'm not so hot on them, either."

He watched her carefully and she watched him right back. If she was here to be the loving wife, she'd better get her act together.

"You know that first summer when Jack and I worked together and I heard he was married, I thought it was a joke. We'd worked side by side twelve hours a day for a week and he never said a word about you."

"Are you trying to start a fight?" she asked.

"No." Oliver leaned against the banister, looking like a man settling in for a long chat. A chat she had no interest in. "But when I asked him about you, he wouldn't shut up. I heard about when you were a baby and your family first moved to his ranch. I heard about how you followed him around as soon as you could walk, snuck into the bed of his truck when he drove away to college."

"What is your point?"

"He said you were his best friend."

Her throat tightened up and she angled her face toward the wind, the breeze cooling her burning eyes.

And that's all I'll ever be.

"What's going on, Mia?" Oliver asked. "I've never asked. I figured whatever relationship you two had worked for you—but something is wrong. It's all over your faces."

It was hard, but she didn't look away or flinch.

The tension inflated inside her like a balloon, and she couldn't get a deep breath. But she didn't say anything. There was nothing to say.

"You don't let anyone in, do you?" he finally asked.

Just Jack, she thought, *and that didn't end so well.*

"Don't be dramatic, Oliver," she said.

"I'm not, I'm simply putting my underused and underappreciated sensitive people skills to work."

She laughed, the tension escaping. The relief was so great she couldn't stop laughing.

"That's more like it," he said, grabbing two more glasses of wine from a passing waiter. "Now, let's have a party."

By the time Jack found them, Mia was doubled over with laughter listening to Oliver's story about Jack eating bugs as the guest of honor in a family's hut.

"He was picking legs out of his teeth for two hours!" Oliver said, and Mia screamed, imagining it.

"Oliver is exaggerating." Jack's familiar low voice sent goose bumps down her arms and over her chest. Her laughter died in her throat, the tension back in force.

Her stomach was never going to be the same.

"Don't listen to him, Mia. You have my word," Oliver said, putting his hand over his heart, "every syllable is the truth."

Jack sighed and leaned against the balcony next to Mia. Static leaped between them, small currents zipping along her skin letting her know just how close he was.

And how far away.

"This night is miserable," he said, tilting his head back.

"Because you don't hang out with the right people," Oliver said, winking at Mia. "Did you make anyone mad in there?" Oliver asked Jack.

"Probably," she said.

Jack looked at her. "How much have you had to drink?" he asked.

"Are you going to scold me?" she asked.

"No." He raised his hand and one of the ever-present waiters appeared. "I'm going to join you."

"I'd better do some damage control," Oliver said. "You two have fun."

The silence left in Oliver's wake was thick and heavy, and she wanted to collapse under the weight. The sheer volume of all the things they weren't saying.

"You remember fun?" he asked and she knew he was looking at her. Her skin felt raw under his gaze.

She nodded.

"I think the last time I had fun was your high school graduation."

"Come on, isn't Africa fun?"

"Fun?" He laughed, but it wasn't joyful.

"No, Africa is hard work and a bureaucratic nightmare."

She wasn't all that shocked to hear it. His emails had been increasingly rant-related.

"But your high school graduation?" His eyes twinkled. "Remember?"

She would never forget. "You drove all night from Cal Poly only to get me out of bed and drag me to the roof of the high school."

And at dawn he drove her home and left— back to college—without once talking to his family. Without even stepping foot in the house.

"Oh, like I had to drag you," Jack said with a laugh, and her body shook at the sound. "You jumped into my truck. And, if I remember correctly, you led the way up to the roof."

"Only because you showed me."

"That was probably a mistake. I spent a lot of sleepless nights in college sure you'd fallen or hurt yourself."

"I never went up on those roofs without you," she said.

"Really?" he asked, looking down at her in surprise.

Jack had this thing, growing up, whenever he got a chance to get into town, he would sneak around Wassau, finding his way up onto the roofs of every public building. The high school, the grocery store, the two churches.

He could walk from Second Street down Main Street without ever touching the sidewalk.

When she started following him around like a lost dog and he realized he couldn't shake her, he took her to the roofs with him.

A whole other world existed up there. He had little forts with sleeping bags and food. Flashlights and books. Sometimes, he'd told her, he slept on those roofs.

His home away from home.

He had a thing for adventure, even then.

She just had a thing for him.

But once he was gone, the roofs were just roofs.

"I can't believe you never got caught," she said.

"Mom found out," he said, his smile fading.

"Really?" she breathed. "I never knew that."

He nodded. "The second night I did it," he said. "I was fifteen and Dad took me into town while he had a beer at Al's and I fell off the grocery store, came home with my clothes all torn."

"What did your mother do?"

Because tearing clothes and climbing buildings weren't something Victoria would let pass, and Victoria had been fond of punishment. Jack shot Mia a dubious look, which hid more pain than she could imagine. "What she always did."

She didn't say anything, didn't offer any sympathy, because he hated that. Always had.

And she respected his wishes. If he didn't want to talk about Victoria's temper, about the abuse, that was his business.

Besides, the night was a big enough bummer as it was. Scandals. Affairs. Divorce. Painfully high heels. They didn't need to stroll down memory lane with Victoria McKibbon.

"You hungry?" he asked, standing upright as if jerking himself away from his thoughts.

"Starving."

"Stay here," he said. "I'll be right back."

TEN MINUTES LATER, Jack made his way toward her with a bottle of red wine under his arm, two glasses sticking out of his coat pocket and a heaping plate of food in his hands.

The twinkle in his eye—that twinkle that she'd recognize if he was eighty years old and disfigured in some terrible accident, that twinkle that led her heart places it had no business going—was like a siren song, leading her astray.

Get ready, that twinkle said, *because I'm coming for you. And I've got a plan.*

In the past that plan usually involved a ladder and a rooftop scheme.

Her heart lurched at the sight of him. At the memory of who he'd been to her.

"You want to go on the roof?"

"Do we need a ladder?"

"Nope."

She blinked, looking around the glittering party that was all for him, and saw just how far he'd come from the roofs of Wassau. And how much she didn't belong here.

"Jack," she whispered, "I'm sure you have plenty of people here you need to schmooze."

He sighed, but the twinkle didn't diminish. "You're probably right."

"See—"

"But I don't care," he said. "I want you to come up to the roof with me."

She'd had just enough to drink to know that going up there wasn't a good idea. She was sad and nostalgic and turned on by the sight of his hand around the bottle of wine.

But she was Mia and he was Jack, and the years and memories between them were a hard knot of grit and rock that neither of them could forget or gloss over.

There was a lot they needed to talk about. His dad, Walter. The ranch and the rough winter they'd had. The financial problems that only seemed to get worse every time she turned around.

"Come on, Mia," Jack said, that twinkle turning into something far more persuasive. "Let's go."

And that was it. Five years after marrying him, she was throwing her hat in with the devil.

The problems could wait.

Tonight wife, she reminded herself. Tomorrow divorce.

CHAPTER THREE

JACK SWIPED a key card and opened the door to a secluded rooftop patio.

"That kind of seems like cheating," she grumbled.

"You expected something else?"

"A little breaking and entering, yeah," she said, following him to a cold fire pit surrounded by single and double chaise longues.

"I've changed my ways," Jack said, and she snorted.

"You don't believe me?"

"I've known you my whole life, Jack. And you don't change."

"Well, neither do you," he said. "Pick a seat, any seat."

Mia didn't play coy. She took one of the doubles, setting down the plate of food he'd given her to hold and he sat down next to her.

His was a living heat, an electric presence, and her body woke up with a tingle and a start.

The Swiss Army knife he pulled out of his pocket looked as if it could launch rockets. He popped open the wine.

"You sure you should leave the party?" she asked. "I mean, it's kind of your shindig."

"I did my part. Oliver can handle it from here." He handed her a glass of wine, her fingertips brushing his and as stupid as it seemed—as high school and clichéd—a zing ran through her blood, warming her from her toes to her hair and everywhere in between.

"Besides," he added, "this might be my last night with my wife."

He said it as a joke, but she didn't laugh.

"You're going back next month," she said, glad it didn't sound like an accusation.

He nodded. "One of the drills broke and we need to see what happened. Might be a problem with the mechanism, in which case all the pumps might malfunction at some point. Or it could be tampering by the militia."

Something in Jack's voice sounded beaten

and she'd never heard that when he talked about his work.

"Aren't you excited about going back?" she asked.

"Excited?" He smiled down at the food. "That's not the right word. Resigned, maybe."

"Because of the militia?"

"Because nothing ever changes there," he said. "We do work and go back a few months later to do the same work all over again. I'm just…tired. I think."

"You need a break," she said. "You could come home—"

"Home, as in the Rocky M?"

She nodded, and he laughed. "That's your home, Mia. Not mine. Never mine."

He turned to her, put his hand on her wrist and her body burned at the contact. "Even with a divorce," he said, "if something happens to me, you'll still have power of attorney. And when Dad dies, the ranch will go to you."

She gasped, turning to face him head-on. "Jack, come on, that's your land. Your family's land."

"You think I care?" he asked. "It's always meant more to you than me."

"But with your parents gone—"

He shook his head. "The memories are bad, Mia. Except for you, nothing good happened there. It's yours. It's why we got married."

She snorted before she could help it. The wine, the emotion, the anger she wanted to pretend she didn't feel—they all coalesced into something sharp and painful.

"It was about your mom," she said, knowing that was the truth, even though she'd spent years trying to pretend it wasn't. "About getting back at her. Beating her at something."

"She had no right to try to kick your family off the ranch after your dad died," he said through his teeth.

"She lost it," Mia agreed, remembering those months when her life was being shredded at the seams.

"And Dad certainly wasn't about to stop her." He shrugged. "What else could we do? Getting married was the right thing."

The truth was she didn't really need to marry him. Her sister, Lucy, and mother, Sandra, had already made plans to leave the ranch. To move to Los Angeles where Lucy would have more success with her jewelry and Sandra could mourn the death of her husband away from the home they'd created on the Rocky M.

And Annie Stone, at the spread nearby, had heard about Mia's troubles and offered her the foreman job on the spot. Mia would have been fine. Perhaps not happy, an employee on someone else's property instead of the land she'd grown up on, but she would have survived.

But Jack had proposed marriage and her heart had answered.

"Eat something," he said, digging into crab cakes with gusto. She grabbed a skewer of beef with satay sauce and leaned back against the cushions.

"I could get used to this," she said.

"Yeah, well, it beats your cooking."

"Slander, Jack. I'll have you know I've improved."

"Really?" he asked.

He glanced over his shoulder at her, and his eyes glittered, traveling quickly down her body as if he hoped she wouldn't notice the trespass.

She noticed, all right. And she liked it.

"I think—" he cleared his throat and went back to staring at his food "—the last time you cooked for me, you burned the pot you tried to boil water in."

"I was twelve, and the last time you cooked for me—"

"Was the night we were on top of the Methodist Church during that rainstorm. I gave you all my beef jerky," he said. "And went hungry. So, don't go complaining."

They drank and ate under a canopy of stars.

The roar of the ocean and the faint hum of the party a few floors below wrapped them in a cocoon, insulating them from the world.

Her body was flush, warm. Alive for the first time in ages. Five years of marriage, thirty years of friendship and her body still tuned to him like a radio. There were so many things they needed to talk about—his father being top of the list—but she didn't want to fight. There would be plenty of time for that tomorrow.

The stars, the wine, the heat in her body all said tonight was for something else entirely.

Jack grinned at her over his shoulder, some kind of relish stuck to his mouth. She used her thumb to wipe his face. So very, very aware of the rough growth of his beard, the soft damp heat of his lower lip.

They were lips that had touched hers once, when the judge told Jack to kiss her. A kiss that was desperate, grateful and scared.

She wanted him to kiss her again, as a woman.

The air between them was humid, and his eyes clung to hers. All those things she thought she should say about safety and being careful were chased away by the look in his eyes.

Every coherent thought scattered like startled birds.

"Why didn't you divorce me before?" he asked.

"Why didn't you divorce me?" she asked right back.

"When we got…married," he finally said, the word seemed sticky on his tongue and she went so still, listening to him, she couldn't even breathe, "we never talked about divorce. I didn't know what you wanted and I didn't…I didn't want to make your life harder or cause you trouble. I always thought that if you filed, I'd sign. No question. But you… never filed. And then life went on."

It sounded so reasonable when he said it. Life went on.

"That's how I felt, too," she whispered. "I wasn't going to thank you for everything by divorcing you if that wasn't what you wanted."

It wasn't the total truth, but he didn't need the total truth. He needed to believe he'd been a hero and she needed to keep her love a secret.

"I wanted you to be safe," he said. "You and your mom. Lucy."

"And we were, Jack. You helped make us safe." She smiled, gratitude a full balloon in her chest. "Thank you."

He watched her for a long time, and she wondered what thoughts were twirling around that big old brain of his.

"You're so beautiful," he whispered, and her head jerked sideways.

"Jack—" she whispered, embarrassed.

"All night I looked over at you, expecting to see Mia, the kid who used to ride horses and herd goats. Who threw punches better than the guys on the football team and never backed down from a fight."

"Everyone grows up," she said, her mouth dry, her palms sweaty.

"Not like you, they don't. I told myself I'd never..." He stopped and she held her breath.

"Never what?" she asked.

His smile was so male and sexy. "Never ask for more than you were willing to give," he murmured.

He had no idea how much she was willing to give.

Kiss me, she thought, waiting for him to come closer, to press those perfect lips to hers. But he didn't. He watched her until she thought she might die from the tension. From the painful desire spilling through her body.

It hurt to want him like this and have nowhere to take it.

And she realized, she could continue to wait for Jack McKibbon. Or she could start doing things her way.

She leaned forward and kissed him.

He started and she expected him to push

her away, to tell her that he didn't feel that way about her. But he didn't.

His fingertips touched her wrist, curled around her hand, keeping her close.

Oh, she thought. *Oh, he wants me, too.*

It was careful. Soft. Two old friends testing the waters.

His lips were firm, chapped slightly and tasted of yogurt and mint. He smelled like everything good and warm in the world. Sun-baked pine needles and clothes fresh from the laundry.

She held her breath, keeping the moment close, memorizing every detail of this kiss. The electric distance between them. The way his nose bumped her cheek, how his lips parted and his tongue tasted the corner of her mouth.

A sigh slipped from her and she let him in.

He pushed the plate of food onto the ground and she tossed the skewer of meat over her shoulder so she could get her arms around him.

Jack McKibbon in her arms.

Solid and heavy. Real.

She held him hard, her fingers finding

the curves of these new muscles of his. The jacket got in the way and she pushed her hands under it, feeling the heat of his skin through his white shirt. He was so hot. So alive.

This was better than every fantasy she ever had about him. Even the ones she tried to forget.

His tongue stroked her mouth, her teeth and lips. He shifted, rearranged himself, so he could hold her tighter, kiss her deeper.

"Mia," he breathed, his fingers toying with the hem of her dress and the painfully sensitive skin of her leg just under it.

She felt every brush of his hand on that inch of skin as if he were stroking her naked body. Just how long it had been since someone touched her came hammering home and her body practically levitated with lust.

It had been a long, long time.

Mia was thirty years old. A wife who'd never been a wife, with only one terrible night of lovemaking she wished she could forget.

All of that was about to change. Right now.

She kissed him hard, pushing him back

against the cushions. Yanking at the buttons of his shirt until something gave and she could finally—oh, yes, yes!—get her hands on the smooth skin of his chest. The muscles of his stomach. He groaned, deep and low in his throat as if the animal in him were coming alive, and that's what she wanted. His hands, not gentle now, slid up under her dress, cupped her ass and squeezed.

She moaned, wanting more. Wanting rough. Wanting everything.

But he leaned back, breaking the kiss, leaving her panting above him.

"I don't want you to think that I am in any way reluctant to do this," he said, arching slightly against her so she knew how not reluctant he was. "But…" His eyes searched hers in the moonlight, liquid and knowing. "Are you sure?"

She nearly laughed. She was wet and hot and dying.

So, *sure* just about covered it.

"We never had a wedding night," she whispered, watching his mouth and wanting it on her breasts, between her legs.

"No," he said, with a slow grin that made

her body clench and shiver. "We never did."

His eyes froze her. Locked her in place, aching against him.

He slid his hands out from under her dress to find the small zipper under her arm and pulled it down. The rasp was loud in the electric silence between them. The dress bagged, and he put a finger under a sleeve, lowering it oh so slowly until the dress caught on her breasts.

He blinked, the heat banked for a second. "Mia," he whispered as if asking permission and her breath clogged in her throat.

She hated her breasts. Heavy and full. Painful at the end of the day and they always, always attracted too much attention.

But right now, Jack's hand trembling against her shoulder, she saw the upside.

She pushed herself away from him and when he moved to sit up, as if the night were over, she pushed him back down.

"Get comfortable," she said and that smile slid back on his lips. Confident and sexy, he lay on his back, tucking his hands behind his head. Waiting for her to make the next move.

Lifting her skirt up nearly to her waist, she straddled his hips, notched herself against the ridge under his fly and they both groaned, twitching hard against the other.

He lifted his hands to her waist, dragging her slowly up and down his erection. Oh, it was so good. So perfect and delicious. The tension in her belly got hotter, harder.

Not yet, she thought. She wanted this to last all night. All night for the rest of her life. She pushed away his hands and shook back her hair, feeling powerful and womanly. Alive in all the very best ways.

And Jack, sweet Jack, just like when they were kids, kept his eyes glued to her face as if looking at her body would be disrespectful. She lifted her hands to her dress and eased the straps off her shoulders.

Jack swallowed, the smile gone now, his lips parting, his eyes wide in wonder.

She reached back and undid her bra, very aware of the revealing moonlight. Of the fact that this was Jack between her legs. Her husband. The man who'd married her and then walked away as if she and everything she loved were nothing. He'd spent the last five years being pursued by deans' wives and probably gorgeous African women and foreign professors with giant brains and reasonable chests.

Self-consciousness crept in where she didn't want it.

"You're beautiful," Jack said, snapping her attention away from her own head games. His eyes were serious. His face—the face of her best friend—earnest. "Whatever you're thinking right now, I need to tell you that I have never seen anything in the world as beautiful as you."

True or not, line or not, it was exactly what she needed to hear.

She dropped her dress and the bra and felt the warm breeze, the starlight, Jack's gaze across her pale skin. Her nipples hardened in a painful cold rush.

"Oh, Mia," he groaned, sitting up, folding her in his arms, his hands cupping her breasts, his eyes aglow. He kissed the trembling skin under her collarbone and worked, in some sort of bizarre migratory pattern, south.

Her skin blazed, every part of her thrumming with pleasure so bright and hot it almost hurt. His mouth was wet against her and all she could think was, *This is Jack. Jack's mouth on my breast. His hand in my hair. His breath against my skin.*

His arms cupped her hips, his fingertips curving around her to find the damp crease that wept at his touch. She arched and he tipped them over, picking her up and shifting her into the center of the chaise. She felt a moan ripple out of her, turned on by all that blatant strength.

He leaned over her, huge and manly. His hands cupped her breasts, pushing them together, and he pressed hot, openmouthed kisses against them.

"I used to dream about you like this," he said and chuckled against her nipple. "A lot, actually."

She arched her back so her nipples brushed his lips. He licked and nipped at them with the sharp edge of his teeth. She groaned, rolling into him, seeking every pleasure center she could find, every point of friction between her body and his.

"Couldn't have been any more than I thought of you like this," she whispered.

"You're kidding," he said, stopping.

She shook her head. There was nothing more she could say.

I've loved you my whole life, she thought.

"Jack." She sighed. "Please—"

His eyes burned in the darkness, and for a moment she thought he realized her inexperience. But then he blinked and his hands gathered her close.

And suddenly everything changed. The banked fires blazed out of control, the hum in her blood turned into a roar. The gentle press of Jack's lips turned firm, hard. His lips didn't kiss, they sucked, and his teeth bit. Mia groaned, pushing and pulling him closer to her.

He yanked at her dress, pulling it off her legs. His fingers found the edge of one of the ridiculous thongs her sister bought for her every birthday and he traced its edge as far as it would go and then back again.

"So naughty," he breathed in her ear. "I had no idea."

Shocks and sparks exploded between her legs, behind her eyes.

He shrugged off his jacket and she helped

get rid of his shirt, tossing it away—a white flag against a black night. His belt clanked in the quiet and his pants rustled to the ground and she didn't even get a chance to look at him before he was back on the chaise with her. All that hot warm skin against hers. The hair on his legs was thrilling, and she ran her feet up the sides of his shins, opening her thighs so he could slip between them.

Bitterness and regret, along with a desperation she didn't know she felt, slipped into her head.

One night, she thought, growing out of control and emotional. *One night.*

Suddenly she was frantic to somehow start and end it all, eager to have this moment over and done with. So she could turn it over and over in her mind back on the ranch.

Memories of Jack were always easier to deal with than reality.

That tension low in her belly, aching between her legs, began to demand release and his fingers slid over her and then, slowly, so, so slowly into her.

She sobbed with pleasure. With pain. With nostalgia and love and years of disappointment.

"Mia?"

"More," she said.

More so she couldn't think. Just feel. More so she couldn't hate him and love him all over again.

He was saying something, but she didn't want to talk. Talking put space between them, allowed thoughts to grow, gave her too much room to think and agonize. To look into his eyes and see the boy who'd married her and walked away.

She reached between them, cupped her hands around the hard length of him. He throbbed in her palm and he hissed hard through his teeth. She lifted her lips, scooted her legs wide.

"I don't have—"

"Shut up, Jack," she whispered.

"No. Mia, I don't have a condom."

She blinked and blinked again. He didn't know.

"I've been on the pill since I was sixteen," she said. Once boys started looking at her funny, and those breasts she hated made their appearance known, Mom had taken no chances, and dragged Mia to the doctor.

"Really?" he asked.

She didn't bother answering, she just guided him home.

They both cried out, shaking against each other. She hadn't realized how big he was, how he would fill her to the point of pain. She took a deep breath, controlling the sting and burn of his flesh splitting hers.

"Mia?" Again that question, the half knowledge that she wasn't a virgin, but not by much, was back in his eyes.

She wrapped her legs around his hips, pulling him so close there was no air between them. He pressed his head to her shoulder, his breath shuddering over her breasts.

"You're killing me. Honestly, honey, we should talk or—"

She squeezed him, using every internal muscle she knew how to control, and he groaned, wrapping his arms around her. His hips, beginning to push against her, slide back and push again. He rearranged her a little, lifting her slightly so when he pulled away she saw stars and that tension in her belly filled her chest. Her head.

"Oh!" She sighed, her breath broken, her body taking flight.

"I don't know why you're doing this," he groaned. "But I can't stop. I can't—"

"Don't!" she cried, scared he would when she needed him so badly to keep going. "Don't stop. Don't…I—"

He lifted his head, his face blocking out the world, and she had no choice but to stare deep into his eyes, right at the boy she loved.

"I've got you," he breathed, and she exploded into the night.

"WHAT THE HELL," Jack muttered, evaluating himself in the mirror over the sink in the small bathroom off the patio. He looked punch-drunk. His hair all over the place, his lips swollen, his eyes glowing and…happy?

"You," he told his reflection, "are a lucky son of a bitch."

Mia. Good God, sweet Mia.

He never expected his five years of abstinence to end in quite this way—not that he was complaining.

No. No complaints here. He smiled again, rolling his shoulders and feeling the delicious weight of his own body. He felt like he owned his skin again. Over the past five years he hadn't given much thought to his celibate life. There was always plenty of work to do and as unconventional as their relationship was, marriage, he figured, was marriage.

If he wasn't having sex with his wife, he wasn't having sex.

But he couldn't totally get his head around what had just happened.

Didn't know if he ever could.

The *why* of it bothered him. Why tonight? Why after talking about divorce? And something about the desperate way she'd pushed him inside her body rankled, too. She'd been so tight.

His hands stilled on the buttons of his shirt. Something sad turned over in his stomach.

Divorce? Now?

Nothing made sense. Which was the theme of the night, he guessed. Before tonight, his relationship with Mia had been the one constant in his life he didn't question. She'd needed him, he'd married her and that was that. And now in one night, she'd told him she wanted a divorce and they'd made love.

He had a thousand questions. And as much as he wanted to throw her over his shoulder and carry her back to their suite to do it all again with a couple of variations, he needed some answers first.

She won't like that, he told himself.

And he knew that if it came down to those variations or getting the answers he needed, he'd forget about the questions.

It had, after all, been five years.

He skipped the two buttons Mia had ripped off in her enthusiasm and did his best to slick back the worst of his haywire hair.

There was no helping it, though; he looked like a man who had been well and truly laid.

By his wife.

He laughed and pushed open the door, stepping back out into the night. And perhaps it was his imagination but it seemed the air still smelled like sex and spice and Mia.

"Mia?" he called, but the quiet was deep around him.

He went over to the women's room and knocked on the door.

No answer. A trickle of unease slid through his caveman bliss.

No, he thought, *she wouldn't.*

But she would. Mia Alatore did whatever she wanted.

He pushed open the door to the women's room, checked every stall, but it was empty. As was the patio.

He ran back downstairs to the party, not believing she'd actually go there, but the alternative was even more unbelievable.

"Oh-ho, Jack," Oliver said, pulling Jack right back out of the party into the empty foyer. "You don't want to go in there, right now."

"Why? Is Mia—"

"Not there, but, Jack, you look a bit—" Oliver tilted his big bald head "—undone. And while I might appreciate a good husband-and-wife reunion, there are those here who would not."

Jack stepped away, panic hammering him hard.

"If you see Mia—"

"I'll send her along."

Jack held hope in his chest like a lantern in the dark. She must have gone to the suite. Of course. Perfect sense.

He ran across the path. His heart pounding; be there, be there, be there.

But the suite was empty. Her duffel bag gone.

Mia had left.

CHAPTER FOUR

Six weeks later

MIA REACHED THROUGH the open driver's-side window of her truck and grabbed the gasket for the well she was in the high pasture to replace.

Twilight was coming down on the far mountains, splashing pink and gold across the endless sky. It was getting warmer up here in the foothills of the Sierras; a thaw was in the air.

Green grass clawed its way up out of ice and snow. Leaves battled it out on the trees. Spring was fighting the good fight against the last of winter.

After calving started, they'd move the cows up here, where they'd summer with the cooler temperatures, the greener grass. But in order to do that, they needed the well working.

And right now it was definitely not working.

Anxiety and anger tugged at her stomach. So much to do at the Rocky M and for the first time since she'd been foreman, she hadn't been able to hire extra seasonal guys. There just wasn't enough money. So it was her and her skeleton winter crew. She was tough and they were good, but everything was stretched thin.

She'd come back from Santa Barbara six weeks ago to a phone call from the bookkeeper. Walter hadn't filed taxes last year, their accounts were frozen and the current taxes were due. Things had been tight before, but now it was downright dire.

The Rocky M wasn't going to make anyone rich, Mia knew that. But she hadn't expected to sink into bankruptcy. And it felt as though, unless she was able to put the brakes on this downward slide, bankruptcy was where everyone was headed.

She knew it was just a matter of getting the new calves to market, but Walter didn't seem to fully grasp all he'd done or hadn't done. Lost in the haze of his sickness, drinking too much and saying nothing at all—Walter was half the man he used to be.

And none of the rancher.

The wind howled over the high land, the ends of her ponytail whipped into her eyes, stinging her face. She wrestled the hair into the collar of her coat, and climbed over to the round corrugated metal fence that protected the well and pump mechanism from snow and wind.

She pumped the handle, and while the gears screeched as they had screeched for years, no water came out.

She really hoped it was a gasket issue—because that was the extent of her well knowledge. She pulled the wrench from the pocket of her canvas barn coat and crouched, her feet sinking in the mud, and wiped the grit and mud from the pump with her numb fingers.

Her neighbor, Jeremiah Stone, who shared this well, knew even less than she did about pumps. Walter usually fixed these problems but…she shook her head, resentment flooding her. Walter was his own problem now.

Her head pounded and her stomach

growled. Two more hours of work before she could head back to the ranch. At least.

Sure would be handy to have Jack around.

Before she could stop herself she glanced up at the ghostly sliver of moon in the eastern sky and wondered where he was.

If he was safe.

Mia shoved her mind away from the thought—from all thoughts of Jack. Those wedding-night memories she thought she'd mull over through the cold, lonely nights, were sharp—too painful to hold. The tenderness and heat, the touch of his hands, the shocking intimacy of his body inside hers—it hurt to think about it.

It hurt and it made her angry.

Angry at him. Herself. The situation. Everything.

And the anger simmered, boiled right under the surface of her skin. In her head. Her stomach. She lived with it. Ate with it. Stared at the ceiling in bed every night and burned with it.

There had been a barrage of emails from him in the weeks after she left. She opened one and deleted the rest—because that first one, full of concern and worry—had been too much.

Now he was concerned. *Now* he was worried. She'd been his wife for five years and the night they had sex, he finally got involved.

Not that she expected anything different. That night wasn't something Jack would take lightly. Jack was about as honorable as they come. Sure, he was absentminded and thoughtless at times, but the guy hadn't taken their vows lightly. That he'd been celibate for five years, while shocking in theory, didn't really surprise her.

That he'd finally slept with her was surprising.

Of course, she'd all but ripped off her clothes.

And as his email subject lines got more and more worried and finally started to get angry, it was easier to delete them without reading them. But then the emails slowed and finally, nine days ago, they stopped.

Mia forced herself to stay away from the news. She'd been too busy to see a divorce lawyer since coming back to the Rocky M, but in her heart it was over between them.

And now she had no idea where Jack was. If he was okay. If his last trip had been successful.

She had nothing.

As she had for the past six weeks since grabbing her clothes and running away from Jack and the rooftop patio, she buried all those memories, her anger and every one of her fears in the endless work that came with the Rocky M.

"YOU OKAY, Jack?"

Jack barely heard Devon Cormick, who'd driven him from Los Angeles to the Rocky M, a mile outside of Wassau. He stared at the sprawling brown ranch house, the thin trail of smoke that rose from the chimney into the darkening sky. The building sat in the shadows of a granite cliff.

The house he'd grown up in always looked in imminent danger of being crushed.

Home, he thought, the word foreign in his head.

The painkillers he'd taken once he got off the airplane in Los Angeles were still kicking around his system. The world felt thick and fuzzy, and he knew being here was dangerous. Dangerous in a way that Darfur couldn't even dream of being.

"I'm fine," Jack said. Though he wasn't. Wouldn't ever be again.

"Are you sure you won't reconsider?" Devon asked. "You could stay with us. Claire would—"

Jack shook his head. His throat was on fire.

"It will die down," Devon said. The young man leaned forward over the steering wheel. The bruises at his temple and across his face were yellowing. One of the explosions had tossed him into the air like a rag doll, throwing him headfirst against one of the fences. It was a miracle his neck hadn't been snapped. "The papers, the university. It can't go on like this."

But his hundred-yard stare out the front window said he wasn't so sure.

Their return from Sudan and their survival of the military's brutal attack had put Devon and Jack in the papers from coast to coast. And it wasn't just the media; the university was all over him, too.

The dean had been inside Jack's house when he got home. As if he had the right, much less a key. And the way he demanded answers—Jack wouldn't argue, the university had a right to those. But they didn't have a right to him. He wasn't his pump. He wasn't the damn drill.

The university didn't own him.

The attention was relentless. But for Devon, the attention would die down—innocence, after all, had its advantages.

For Jack, the questions would come at him for the rest of his life.

Do you remember the attack?

Why were you beyond the perimeter of the compound?

What happened to Oliver Jenkins?

Jack flinched and shut his eyes. The morphine burned in his pocket, a promise, a sweet whisper of how good forgetting could be.

"I can't leave you here. I'll take you back to the university," Devon said. He put the car in gear and turned in the front seat ready to reverse down the long driveway.

"I'm staying," Jack said, his voice a thin wheeze. The doctors had told him not to talk to keep from irritating his damaged throat.

But Devon liked conversation. Another reason not to go home with him.

"But you're pretty far away from a hospital, and with—"

Jack opened the door, and Devon shut up, putting the car in Park and hurtling out the driver-side door to help Jack out of the car.

It was hard with his knee and the broken hand.

"What about physical therapy?" Devon asked. "For your hand?"

Jack ignored him, swinging his duffel bag up over his good shoulder with his good hand.

"Jack! You need to talk to someone about Oliver, about what happened. You can't just—"

"Thanks for the ride, Devon."

Devon sighed, wiped a hand over his eyes. "Christ, you're stubborn."

Jack would have laughed if it hadn't felt like swallowing glass.

"Fine. Is there anyone here who will take care of you?" Devon asked.

Jack looked at the brown house with the dark windows. It blended into the forest, the granite outcrop—a shadow in twilight.

No one had ever taken care of him here before.

Except Mia.

Anger burned through him like a gasoline fire, hot and quick and greasy. She'd left him on that hotel rooftop, run away like a child, didn't return a single email or phone call for four damn weeks and then, after the bombings, after…Oliver, still nothing.

Where the hell were you, Mia? he thought.

The only things he could count on were the pills in his pocket, the nightmares and that no one would find him here.

"You better go," he told Devon. "The pass gets dangerous in the dark."

Devon looked sufficiently nervous at the idea and Jack bit back a smile. He'd watched the man's fingers get whiter and whiter on the steering wheel on the way over the mountains.

"If you're sure?"

Jack nodded. He wanted a get this over with—walk through those doors, face down the demons and then sleep. For two months, until he was forced back to San Luis Obispo to answer the dean's questions.

He barely heard Devon drive away as he took the gravel pathway up to the house. Why were the lights off but the fireplace going? It was getting close to seven o'clock and at least the lights in the kitchen should be glowing, with some traffic coming from the bunkhouse to the dining room.

The barn to his left was silent. One brown gelding was in the nearby corral.

It was spring and the place looked like a ghost town.

The front door creaked open under his fist and he helped his left knee up the front stoop and entered the house.

He found a weak fire, mostly glowing embers, in the living room fireplace, but the house was cool. The furnace was off. It was eerie.

A vicious snapshot, a horrific memory of the pump site, the compound, blackened to cinder. Nothing but craters and smoke where people and equipment used to be.

He shook his head, clearing the image, jarring it loose.

A light flicked on in the kitchen and he heard thumping in the mudroom.

"Damn it!" Unmistakably Mia.

He dropped his bag and stepped into the wide-open dining room, waiting for his reckoning.

GOOD GOD, could no one do anything around here but her? Mia wondered, toeing off her boots. The left one stuck, a reminder she needed to get some new ones, and she bent over to pull it off, leaning against the cold walls of the mudroom.

The furnace wasn't on. It had to be the damn pilot light, and Walter either hadn't noticed or hadn't bothered getting anyone to check.

It was seven o'clock. She was starving. Tired to the bone. And did not want to deal with the thirty-year-old furnace.

"Walter!" she yelled, coming into the dining room. She tossed her truck keys into the dish that had sat for years on the counter that divided the huge open kitchen from the dining area. One glance into the kitchen and she noticed that the guys had cleaned up after their dinner.

Thank God for small blessings.

The light on the slow cooker was still on

so she had to hope there was some chili left for her.

"It's freezing in here. Did the pilot light go—"

"Mia."

She turned and froze.

In the shadows, like a ghost, stood Jack.

Her heart lurched and for a second she couldn't breathe. Jack. Here. Shock emptied her head of any thought, any emotion.

But then the heavy load she floundered under lifted for a moment and she wanted to sag against the counter, relief making her dizzy.

He was here. When she needed him most.

"What…" She swallowed. "What are you doing here?"

He frowned. "Hiding out," he said, his voice a harsh rasp. Painful sounding.

"What's wrong with your voice?"

He blinked at her. "You…don't know?"

The bubble of her relief popped and she truly saw him. He was so pale and thin. Too thin. His jacket hung on him. His eyes, his beautiful chocolate eyes, were dim.

His hand was in a cast and a sling, his fingers limp against the blue cloth.

"What happened, Jack?" she asked, unable to keep the panic out of her voice. She crossed the kitchen in a heartbeat and reached for those pale, still fingers, but he shifted away from her. Her hand hung in the air, useless.

"Attacked," he said.

She staggered back, her hand banging against the chair before she got a grip on it.

Attacked. Bile churned through her empty stomach.

Her eyes searched him for more injuries. Obviously there was something wrong with his throat, his arm. Was he holding his weight funny?

"Your leg?" she asked.

"Knee." He watched her. "You didn't know?"

"No," she whispered, looking at him. "Oh, my God, Jack, I didn't know." She reached out again and ignored his flinch, pressed forward when he shifted back. Her fingers landed against his cool cheek, and his eyes, so cold and distant they could have been a stranger's, didn't leave hers.

That night in Santa Barbara blazed between them, a fire that separated them.

He was still angry.

"Jack—"

"Can I stay for a few days?" he asked.

"Of course," she said. "Of course. It's your home."

His smile was bitter. Sharp.

A heavy thud echoed through the house and Mia dropped her hand. Another thud and a slide.

"Mia?" Walter called from the other room and Jack stepped away from Mia, something flickering in his dead eyes. Anger. What else?

"In here, Walter," she called and Mia could see the panic on Jack's face.

He's your father, she wanted to say. *And he's changed. That man you hated isn't here anymore.*

But she didn't say anything. Jack would see soon enough.

An old man, so frail and thin, so utterly diminished that he seemed nearly childlike, pushed a walker into the kitchen.

"Holy shit," Jack breathed, turning away to face the far window. Tension so thick it was like acrid smoke rolled off him, choking the air out of the room.

"What the hell is going on?" Walter asked

through lips that didn't move in a face that didn't move. The facial paralysis was part of his Parkinson's disease. As was the tremble in his arms and hands. And the shuffling gait. All part of the disease that was ravaging his body.

But the smell of booze was his own stupid fault.

"Walter—" she said.

"The pilot light must have gone out on the furnace," the sixty-four-year-old man said. "You need to go down and look at it."

Mia bit her lip so hard she tasted blood.

"Who the hell is this?" Walter asked, turning to look at Jack's back. "We can't hire hands that are injured."

"He's not a hand, Walter," she said, watching Jack stare out the window, his face harder than the granite cliff behind the house.

Finally, he turned, eyes blazing to face his father.

"Jack," Walter breathed. He pitched, unsteady on his feet, and Mia leaned forward to keep him upright. She could feel him shaking so hard it was a wonder he could stand. Tears burned her eyes, for both these men and the pride that kept them so far apart.

"Son—"

Jack flinched at the word.

"You're back," Walter said, his words mumbled and thick. Hard to understand. "Your arm?" Mia could feel Walter shift, his hand lifting as if to touch his son and she wanted to stop him. Protect him. Because Jack was a land mine of hate and anger, and there was no telling what pressure would set him off.

Jack stepped back, away from Walter and Mia. His eyes empty, a foreign wasteland.

Without saying anything, he turned toward the hall leading to the bedrooms.

"Jack," she cried.

But he was gone. Disappearing into the cool, inky darkness of the home he hated.

CHAPTER FIVE

FIRST THINGS FIRST. Mia lit the pilot light and the old furnace rumbled and thumped back to life. And then, because it was eat something or pass out, she grabbed a bowl of chili and went into the den where the computer sat on her desk.

Walter was already there, sitting in the threadbare easy chair by the window.

"Find out what happened," he demanded, pointing a shaking finger toward the computer as if it were a pet he couldn't get to obey.

She sat down and booted up the system, shoveling bites of chili into her mouth while the computer hummed through the start up.

Attacked.

There were so many varying degrees of how bad it could be, that she couldn't actually wrap her head around it. And she didn't want to guess. She'd played the worst-case-scenario game last year while Jack was on sabbatical, and she knew all it did was give her ulcers.

But in the back of her head, in the soft spot on her neck, she felt a chill. Whatever had happened, it was bad enough to send Jack, wounded and wasted, back to Rocky M.

She went immediately to the BBC website and typed in Darfur.

The last article was dated four weeks ago and she clicked on it.

The first headline exploded across the screen and she dropped her spoon: Scientist Killed In Crossfire.

"No," she breathed, panic an animal clawing its way out of her body. "No, no, please, no."

She scanned the article, piecing together information. Searching for Oliver's name. Her brain barely able to process everything.

"Read it," Walter demanded. "Out loud."

"Ahh…" Her voice shook. "'Three hydro-engineers working in tandem with Water for Africa were repairing a broken water well outside the Sudanese city of El Fasher when the Sudanese government broke the cease-fire between itself and rebel militia forces in the area.

"'The area was bombed late last night.

"'Oliver Jenkins, part of the engineering team responsible for the revolutionary drill and well system, was…'" She stopped. The next word, right there in horrible black and white, stuck in her throat. She couldn't say it. Because it couldn't be true. Couldn't possibly.

Not Oliver.

"He dead?" Walter asked. "That Oliver guy?"

That last night, in Santa Barbara, Oliver's laugh had filled the room. His eyes had picked her apart, found her pain and tried to help. He'd seemed, he'd always seemed, somehow larger than life. Larger than all of them.

"Yes," she whispered, her entire body splitting with a grief so hard and horrible it felt like something else. Like anger. Like pain. "He's dead."

"What else does it say?"

Walter was worked up, his eyes damp, his skin red.

"The well was destroyed," she said, finishing

the last of the article. "And surviving engineers Devon Cormick and Jack McKibbon were evacuated to Kenya where they received treatment."

She pushed away from the desk. Her emotions needed action. Her confusion needed answers.

"That's it?" Walter asked. "That's all it says?"

She nodded and before she could think better of it, she turned and headed down the hall toward Jack's old room.

Oliver was dead and Jack had come back like some kind of ghost and she was just supposed to sit back and…what? What the hell was he doing here? What did he want?

She pounded on the door and waited but there was no answer.

"I know you're in there, Jack," she cried, her voice breaking with the tears she was swallowing like so much glass. When he didn't answer she grabbed the knob and turned it. There were no locks on any of the doors, a little leftover from Victoria's reign of terror, and the door slid open across the thick carpet in Jack's old room.

It was bare now. All the posters and music,

the science fair ribbons and rock samples, the stacks of books—all gone. He'd taken them when he left, erasing himself from this house as if he'd never been there.

But Jack sat on his single bed, staring out the bare window at a bright moon.

His sandy hair gleamed in the bruised twilight and Mia's grief outran her, bringing her up short.

"Oliver?" she whispered, and Jack's head bent.

She turned and faced the door frame, biting her lip until the tears drained from her eyes and she could speak.

"What happened?" she asked, pressing her thumb against the notches in the wood that had grown along with Jack when he was a boy.

Jack didn't answer. He sat unmoving, staring at his hands. Silent as stone.

"What the hell happened, Jack!" she cried, circling the bed to face him. He didn't look up and all she saw was the bone-white part in his hair. "He was my friend, too!" she yelled, her fists clenched against the emotions that threatened to tear her to pieces.

Finally, he glanced up and she gasped at

the sight of his eyes. Dry as dirt, but wasted all the same. Ghost eyes. Empty.

"Mia," he breathed, his voice damaged and raw. "Please—"

She saw something pull apart in him, a long string unraveling. And she remembered Oliver and Jack, brothers in a way. Conspirators and teammates. More than friends. As terrible as her grief was, she couldn't imagine what he felt. The loss he carried. Not just his friend, but his life's work. Gone.

"I'm so sorry, Jack. I'm sorry I wasn't there when it happened." She crouched down beside him, careful not to touch him, because she couldn't tell where he wasn't hurt.

His eyes met hers and she searched through those chocolate depths for a sign, a glimmer of the boy she knew, the man she'd loved.

You're there, she thought, all those old feelings she thought she'd banished after Santa Barbara surfacing. *I know you're there and I know you came here for a reason.*

You must feel something for me. You must.

"Leave me alone," he said.

She blinked, rocked back on her heels.

Right. Of course. How could she forget?

Jack didn't need her. He never needed her. Happiness. Grief. Health. Injury. Jack did it all on his own.

"Screw you, Jack," she breathed, and left him there to rot.

WALTER STOOD OUTSIDE his son's bedroom door. Shut for two damn days. Fool boy was going to kill himself.

He wanted to kick the door down, pull that boy up by the scruff and shake him until he started fighting.

Dying without a fight was a shameful way to go.

Walter knew, because he was giving it his best shot.

Hypocrite, he told himself, but the word didn't even leave a mark.

Mia's door opened and she slid out into the hallway. She seemed so small these days, tinier than usual. Which was saying something.

She looked like her mother. As the girlishness left her face and womanhood settled in around the corners of her eyes and lips, the fact that Mia was Sandra's daughter was unmistakable.

Sometimes, in a certain light, after enough to drink, Walter was sure Sandra was back. In his home. Bringing the warmth and laughter that had vanished when she left.

"Did he come out?" she asked, when she saw Walter standing outside Jack's bedroom like a crippled scarecrow, rooted to the spot.

Walter shook his head, gripping the rubber handles on the walker with his useless, trembling hands.

"You should go lie down," she said.

Go lie down. Take a seat. Have a rest.

It was all he ever did.

That and think. And then drink to forget everything he thought about.

"He come here to die?" he asked, nodding toward the door and, behind it, the boy he hadn't seen in more than five years.

Mia had always known Jack better than Walter did and if anyone could answer that, it'd be her.

"He has a sprained knee and a broken hand," she said. "He's hardly about to die."

But Mia's eyes were dark. Her face, pinched and drawn.

They both knew that whatever was wrong with Jack was way worse than a sprained knee.

He'd survived an air raid that had killed his best friend. Walter didn't understand much about what was going on over there in Sudan, or who exactly the bad guys were. They all seemed to be doing their best to blast the country to hell and back.

But Jack, who'd only been trying to bring clean water to a desert, got caught in the middle of it.

"It's the only reason he'd come back here," he said. He knew the truth, had lived with it every day, practically since Jack was born. "Victoria drove that boy away and I let her."

Mia tugged on the sleeve of his old blue sweater. "Come on, Walt. Don't you have some drinking to do?"

He had so many of her sarcastic barbs in his hide, that one glanced right off. He shook his head and she stepped back to stand in front of him. Her eyes were skeptical. "You're not drinking?"

"It's seven in the morning."

"Hasn't stopped you before."

Now that one hurt. Walter didn't say anything, just turned his walker around in tiny increments until he faced the hall leading to the kitchen and dining room.

"Gloria is coming today," Mia said. Gloria came and cleaned up and cooked every other day. Filling the freezer with casseroles and meaty soups to put in the slow cooker, and sweeping and dusting around him in the living room, as if he were just another piece of furniture.

In the kitchen, he watched Mia pour coffee into one of the travel mugs and take a big slice of ham out of a bag in the fridge.

"You want something?" she asked and he nodded, pointing to the coffee.

She grabbed a mug and filled it with black coffee, setting it down beside him as he collapsed into a chair.

He wanted to tell her to sit down, eat a proper meal. But he knew how much work she had to do, and how many hours of sunlight to do it in.

Shame burned through his veins and his fingers twitched, searching out the weight of his whiskey glass.

"I'm sorry," he said and she turned toward him, chewing her meat.

"For what?"

For drinking. For screwing up the money. For getting sick.

"Three days ago," he said. "The pilot light."

Her smile was sad, sweet, and his shame burned hotter. She deserved better. Hell, that boy locked up in his room deserved better. She shoved the last of the ham into her mouth and wiped her hands on a tea towel. Then she grabbed three plastic amber bottles from the windowsill.

"If you're really sorry," she said, plunking the bottles down on the table in front of him, "take these."

Mia grabbed her keys, her beat-up ball cap from the counter and left. Leaving him alone with the medication he refused to take.

Doctors told him Parkinson's wasn't a death sentence. That if he took those pills like he was supposed to, he could have a life.

But it wouldn't be his old life.

No horses. No working cattle. None of the things he'd done and loved forever.

All those things that made him who he was. A cattleman. A tough son of a bitch.

And without the work, who was he really?

He wasn't a husband, hadn't been for a long time. He'd never really been a father. Not much of a father-in-law, either.

He'd been a waste, and the disease was here to put an end to a miserable life.

Without the pills, death crept closer on shuffling feet, its face a thick, unmovable mask.

The booze helped, too.

And Walter went to bed every night knowing he was another day closer to leaving all the shame and the bitter regrets behind. And he liked it that way. The pain was bad, sometimes real bad, and the electrical currents that ran through his body as if he were water were getting worse.

But pain was nothing.

The booze helped with that, too.

Walter sniffed hard and felt the scruff of his beard with a shaking hand. He used to shave every morning, gave the guys a hard time if they didn't.

When did I stop? he wondered. When he first had trouble with his hands, two years ago? When Mia finally made him go to the doctor and get diagnosed a year ago? When he started drinking?

"My boy is back," he said aloud, the words echoing through the empty kitchen. His empty home and life.

Well, he realized, not so empty anymore.

Jack was back for a reason. Signs and shit weren't something he usually believed in, but his son was back, sleeping in the bedroom he'd grown up in.

Victoria, at long last, was gone, and it seemed as if Jack being here now was a chance to make things right between them.

It took a while to wrestle his hands into action, to put them where he wanted them, on the white caps on top of those amber bottles, and it took even longer to open them.

"Damn it," he muttered as the pills scattered away from him, rolling over the table and falling onto the floor. But he got three, a yellow one, a big white one and a small orangish one, cupped in the valley of his palm.

If he lifted his hand, they'd spill from all the shaking, so he bent his head and licked the pills from his palm, tasting the salt of his skin. The bitter medicine.

He swallowed them dry and he turned, five small moves, pulling his ruined body around to go find the whiskey to wash it down. OH, GOD. The heat was terrible. The sun was melting him down like wax.

"Jack!" Oliver cried, and Jack turned to look for him, but he couldn't find him in the dunes. Sand kicked up in his face, the sun blinded him.

I hate Africa, he thought.

"Jack!" Oliver yelled again. "Why didn't you tell anyone the maps were wrong?"

The guilt was a vise around his throat. And he couldn't breathe for the pain.

"I meant to," he gasped. "I did. But Mia—"

"Don't blame her."

"I don't!" he managed to yell past the pain. "I blame myself. It's my fault!"

He woke up with a start, jerking himself upright. Freezing despite his dreams of the desert.

His whole body was drenched in cold sweat.

The morphine beckoned but he ignored it. Looking at his father's face three nights ago, at the ravages alcohol had made in that man, killed the allure of those painkillers.

He wouldn't go down that road. Not if it meant being anything like his father.

He pulled himself from the bed, knowing from weeks of hard experience that once the nightmare woke him up, there'd be no sleeping.

Without turning on the light, he opened his bedroom door and made his way to the bathroom. Hazy moonlight slipped in the window on the far end of the hallway, but Jack didn't need the illumination. Preferred things without it, truth be known. The dark was another layer he wrapped around himself, insulating him from the cold, harsh realities of the outside world.

Realities like Mia. Like his father. Like George Gibson, dean of Cal Poly, who called Jack's cell phone yesterday to remind him of the board meeting in six weeks' time.

Might as well call it a reckoning.

No. He'd take the dark.

The bathroom tiles were cool under his feet and he reached into the shower and cranked on the hot water, tempering it with very little cold.

Hilarious that he dreamed of the desert but couldn't seem to get warm.

Once the shower was steaming he stepped in, the heat scalding his flesh and he gasped, welcoming the pain, until his body got used to it. He braced his hands on the wall of the shower, his cast thunking against the tiles. The plaster was getting wet, but he didn't care.

The hot water beat down on the back of his head, rolling past his ears. He opened his lips and the water was warm on his tongue.

Why are you here? he asked himself and spat out the water.

He thought he'd be able to hide out in peace, but there was no peace here. Not for him.

Christ, his father. He hadn't anticipated how hard it would be to see him like that. Wasted by disease.

And even his old room, empty of every physical reminder of his childhood, was still filled with memories. Few of them worth having.

And Mia, here. The anger wasn't fading. It was an ember in his chest, burning white-hot.

She hadn't even known about the attack.

She hadn't bothered to answer an email or a phone call or, apparently, watch the news. It was as if she'd left every tie to him behind on that roof in Santa Barbara.

While he'd been fighting hideous pain in a Red Cross helicopter with memories of her, she'd been oblivious. Unconcerned. And his anger about her abandonment made him uneasy.

He liked how he knew Mia, who she was to him. He liked the slot she occupied in his life. Wife but not wife. Friend from afar. It made sense.

Sex on a roof didn't make sense. Being here didn't make sense. Being hurt and angry about her didn't make any sense.

What made sense was going back to his condo.

The reporters would be gone at this point. The university would get their pound of flesh in another month and a half. He could shower all night long at his empty apartment in San Luis Obispo. He could torture himself with guilt, staring up at the ceiling over his own king-size bed.

He didn't need to be here anymore.

So why did he stay?

Because you deserve it, a voice said, ugly and insidious.

Water seeped into his cast and the tickle turned to an itch. An itch that spread, as all the itches did. Spread like wildfire, like lice eating his skin. It was making him crazy.

With his good hand he turned off the water and yanked a towel off the rack, tucking it around his waist. He flipped on the light, blinking at the sudden brightness. The drawers in the old oak vanity didn't have any scissors big enough to do the job. The hallway led him to the kitchen, where the big knives were stuck to a magnetic stripe over the stove.

He grabbed the biggest and slid it, sharp side up, under the loose plaster around his forearm. The knife sawed through the plaster, cutting it into ragged chunks. The tip of the knife pierced his skin but he didn't let up because he needed the damn thing off. His leg was better. The cuts were healed. This cast was the last of the desert he still carried on his body and he wanted it gone. Now.

With a gasp he sliced through the last of it, right between his fingers, and the cast fell off like old skin.

He flexed his fingers, twisted his wrist,

scratched all those places he hadn't been able
to get to for the past few weeks. His fingers
scraped through a river of blood, smearing it
over his fingers, across his palm. He watched,
didn't stop until his hands were covered.

"Son?"

He jumped at Walter's voice, dropped his
hands so fast they hit the counter, electric
shots zipping up his arms.

"What?" he asked, turning to rinse his
hands. Collect himself from whatever edge
he seemed to linger on.

"You all right?" Walter shuffled into the
room, his navy robe opening over a pale
chest. Jack could barely see his grizzled face
in the shadows.

It was as if the night was eating him. One
of them, anyway.

"Just fine, Dad," he said, shaking water off
his hands.

He brushed past him in the dark, noticing the damp in the corner of his dad's eyes
reflected the light like diamonds.

A WEEK AFTER Jack's arrival at the ranch,
Mia dismounted Blue in the middle of the
south pasture.

"Heya," she said, shooing some of the heifers away from the well. She pumped fresh water into the three-foot basin and the horse dipped his muzzle into the cool spring water.

Days like this—with the sunshine hot and the breeze cool, with pastures full of healthy cows and the work manageable—were the days she lived for. The days that reminded her that as hard as the work was, this ranch was her happy place.

Always had been.

"Mia." Chris, who'd been at the Rocky M almost as long as her, walked over to where she stood. The dogs, Daisy and Bear, trotted behind the wiry cowboy. Daisy and Bear followed him everywhere. Everyone at the ranch joked that the dogs thought Chris was a lost calf.

Chris was brown from the sun and every year Mia thought he looked more and more like beef jerky. He was all sinew and grit, though his big blue eyes hinted at a hidden softness.

"How are the mothers-to-be?" she asked, looking over her shoulder at the field of pregnant cows. Calving season was right around the corner.

"Fat and happy." Chris tipped his head off his forehead and sighed. "But we're a week out," he said. "Maybe less."

"A week?" Perfect. More than perfect. The sooner those calves were on the ground, the sooner they could be sold and the sooner they'd all be out of this mess. There was a light at the end of the tunnel.

She smiled at Chris.

He frowned back.

Good old Chris. He could find a dark cloud on a sunny day.

"Any chance we can get some more hands?" he asked.

"No," she said, with a sigh. Not in less than a week.

"Old man screwed up good, didn't he?"

Mia didn't say anything. There was nothing to say. And she was trying, damn it, to hold on to her happy day.

"Heard Jack was back. He'd be handy—"

She laughed. She couldn't help it. Even if the sprained knee and broken hand weren't a problem, Jack had barely left his room in five days. She heard him in the middle of the night, taking showers and roaming through the kitchen. She wasn't sure if it was nightmares driving him from his bed, or pain.

She told herself every night that she didn't care. But every night it was a battle to stay in her bed. She'd given him enough of herself over the years—she had nothing left to give.

Chris spit into the dirt, the picture of a disgusted cowboy.

"If you've got something to say," she said, "then just say it."

"It seems to me we're carrying a lot of deadweight around here, Mia. And we can't afford it."

"You think I don't know that?" she asked. She was stuck between a rock and a hard place. The old man wasn't taking his meds, and Jack...hell, Jack was a ghost.

"I'll ask Jeremiah," she said.

Chris nodded after a second, the topic of Jack finished for the moment. "He's a good man with the animals."

She pulled on her gloves and grabbed Blue's reins, happy to be able to solve one immediate problem. "Let's move the heifers over to the pasture with the squeeze chute.

And start feeding them at night. Maybe we can work these calves during the day for once. I'm sick of stumbling out of bed at midnight."

"You and me both, boss," Chris said with a laugh. He whistled and his horse Beans walked up like a big tame dog. Over the small rise, Billy and Tim appeared.

The four of them. Four of them and two dogs working maybe a hundred calves?

She could feel Chris's anxiety a mile away. Even the dogs deserted him, darting across the field toward Billy, who had a ham sandwich in his hands.

"We'll be fine, Chris," she said. "The boys are good. And next year we'll be able to hire all the extra help we need."

"You think?"

She smiled, more optimistic than she'd been in ages, despite the problems in the house. "I'll hire one just to make you smile all day long."

"Better make her pretty."

She laughed, feeling the stress roll away. Everything was going to be okay in the end. What was that saying? If it's not okay, it's not the end?

That could be the motto of the Rocky M.

"I know you're worried, Chris. But everything is going to work out." She pulled herself up onto Blue, who sighed and twitched with pleasure. "You and I have both been here long enough to know that this ranch won't let us down."

The men in that house, not so much.

"I hope you're right." Chris sighed.

"Mia!" A woman's voice yelled from the house and Mia turned to see Gloria on the porch, waving a white dishcloth. "We have a problem."

Oh, brother.

CHAPTER SIX

"He's not here," Gloria said, pushing her glasses up with the back of her wrist. Her hands were slick and Mia didn't want to know if it was chicken guts or some kind of cleaning solution that made them wet. "Hasn't been all day."

Walter's threadbare recliner in the living room sat empty. No half-filled glass at its side. No walker.

No Walter.

A mystery for sure. But hardly one that should bring her in from the fields.

"Is he in bed?" she asked.

"Nope." Gloria shook her head, her long silver-streaked black hair swishing across the back of her purple sweatshirt. "And I'm no nurse. If he's caught in the bathroom again, you go fish him out."

Gloria turned, walking back to the kitchen. Mia watched her leave and braced herself to go find Walter to help him pull his pants up.

Needing a little extra help, she closed her eyes and thought about that notebook she kept of all the places Jack went to for his work. The deserts for digging, the cities for conferences. She scrolled through what she knew and picked Italy.

Italy, because she was starving and would kill for a pizza, and she wouldn't have to deal with her father-in-law, possibly stuck like a turtle on the bathroom floor.

Hell. She'd take the high pasture at this point.

"Good God." Swearing in Spanish because it made her feel better, she stomped out of the living room and down the hall. He'd better have his pants on. Really. But he wasn't in the bathroom. She rechecked his bedroom, and the bed was empty. And made. The barn? On her way down the adjacent hallway she passed the open doorway to the office and stopped. The computer was on, the white light from the screen, illuminating the weathered, bearded face of her father-in-law.

"Walter?"

"Apparently, Cal Poly is having some

kind of board meeting in a month," he said, pointing at the screen. "Jack's supposed to be there. Answer questions about what happened in Sudan."

His fingers, the ones pointing at the screen and the ones securely around the mouse, were shaking, but still…he was using a mouse. That would have been impossible a month ago.

"What are you doing?" she asked.

"Trying to find out what's happening to my son, since he won't come out of his room and tell me."

"No…" She stepped into the room to get a better look at him. His face seemed to have more mobility. He seemed, ridiculously, just a little more like…Walter.

"Did you take your meds?" she asked.

Walter held up his hand, the tremors were there, but his whole hand didn't relentlessly circle. The counterclockwise movement that could wind a watch was gone.

He had taken his meds.

"How many days?"

"Five counting this morning."

The doctors said that within days of taking

medicine regularly there'd be a decrease in symptoms.

Looked like they were right.

"How you feeling?" she asked. She didn't want to be relieved. She didn't want to take this as some kind of sign that maybe, please dear God, maybe things might swing north for a change.

"Can't shit," he said, taking a sip from a glass filled with ice and golden liquid.

She laughed. Walter, it seemed, was back—in some fashion.

Mia turned away, heading back to the kitchen to tell Gloria everything was okay, but she was sidetracked by Jack's shut bedroom door.

Her heart, buoyed by Walter's unprecedented step back into the land of the living, sank again.

She pressed her hand against the wood, and imagined for just a moment that she felt a heartbeat. It was a trick, of course, the rebound of her own pulse bouncing against the wood and back against her skin.

Because it certainly wasn't Jack she felt.

The weight of her grief threatened to pull her under so she walked away from the door. From Jack. And instead thought about Walter. About Walter taking his meds and how things could change around here if he joined the land of the living for good.

It was just enough hope to keep her head above water.

IT WAS A DREAM, she knew it was. The dark, the horses, the sensation of flying. Oliver. None of it could be real.

Wake up, Mia, she told herself.

But she couldn't seem to pull herself free. The dream was quicksand and she was caught.

The horses grew wings and the flying sensation turned into falling and she fought it, fought everything.

"Mia," Jack said and she knew that was a dream, too, because Jack didn't come out of his room.

"For crying out loud, Mia, wake up."

Mia's eyes snapped open and she jerked herself upright, nearly clipping Jack in the chin.

"What's happening?" she panted, adrenaline making a mess of her. There was a problem, right? She needed to do something?

Fix something? She was in the living room, which was weird. Sitting in the recliner with her feet up. Soft light from the reading lamp beside her pooled in the folds of the red blanket over her chest.

"You were having a nightmare," Jack said. He sat on the ottoman next to her feet and she could feel his heat through her wool socks. It was like a dream. Her husband here in the quiet night, tucking a blanket around her shoulders. Waking her from a bad dream.

It was a lingering fantasy from over from a year ago when she'd still gone to bed thinking that this marriage of hers might one day be real.

"Am I now?"

"What?"

"Dreaming."

"No."

"Then what the hell are you doing?"

WHAT THE HELL are you doing, Jack? the voices asked. The voices were annoying. There was a whole damn chorus in his head these days. Not for the first time he considered how the painkillers would shut those voices up.

How the painkillers would make it all go away.

But he still resisted.

"You looked cold," he said and stood, his knee barely twinging. The exercises that he did in his room were improving his range of motion.

Mia sat up, and the red blanket that was pulled up to her neck fell down, revealing the paperwork in her lap he hadn't bothered to move. Calving reports, from what he could tell. She must have dozed off while reading them.

Her eyes had purple shadows under them and he could tell she'd lost weight since Santa Barbara.

This ranch had a way of diminishing people, stripping away anything extra, until all they had was what they needed to survive.

Jack wanted to tell her to leave before this ranch did to her what it did to his mother. His father. What it would have done to him had he stayed.

But he didn't say anything. He didn't have the energy.

And maybe it wasn't his business.

Wife or not, Mia had run away in Santa Barbara.

He didn't know what that made them, but it sure as hell wasn't friendly.

"No, what are you doing out of your room?" she asked, as if he'd escaped from his cage.

"I'm not allowed out?" he asked.

She shot him an acidic look.

"I was getting something to eat." His voice, still rusty from lack of use but no longer raw from the smoke, creaked out from his throat, and he started to walk away.

"Where are your crutches?"

"Don't need 'em."

She grabbed his hand, and while no longer broken, it hurt all the same. Her touch was a fire of its own. But he didn't turn. Didn't want to look at her and feel anything. He wanted to go back to his room, eat a sandwich and fight off sleep.

He wanted the numbness back and he knew that as long as he was around Mia he'd never be numb.

She dropped his hand and he was grateful.

"I left you alone in your room five days ago

to rot." Her voice was sharp and he nearly smiled. "I just never thought you'd actually do it."

"Me, neither," he said and left her and the living room behind, heading for the kitchen and the sandwich he'd put on the counter when he heard her moaning.

The light was on over the stove, creating a warm glow that faded into the dark shadows. He hungered for the dark shadows, the insulation of the night.

"Your hand," she said. "No more cast?"

"I took it off." He looked down at the pale hand and arm. The scabbed-over cut between his fingers.

"Is that smart?" she asked. "Shouldn't you see a doctor—"

"I was told the cast could come off at six weeks. I tore it off at seven."

"Should you be going to a doctor anyway?" she persisted, following him like the kid she'd been. "For checkups or physical therapy or something?"

"I'm fine," he said again, with a little more power behind it. He knew it was a mistake to put that blanket over her. To sit at her feet, even for a few moments, to watch the whirlwind that was Mia Alatore at rest.

"What about medication?" she asked.

Yes! Yes! Yes! The medication, the voices cried.

"Jack, I'm just worried—"

"Worried?" He turned to her. "Really? The woman who didn't answer a single phone call after leaving me on that roof?" He stepped a little closer until she moved back, keeping a cool distance between them that he suddenly wanted to eradicate. "Since you're asking so many questions, how about you answer some, huh?"

Her face got tight, her eyes shuttered. She didn't like being on the other end of the inquisition.

"Why didn't you answer my emails?" he asked. "Or phone calls?"

She swallowed and lifted her chin, as though her show of bravery would hide the white-knuckled hold she had on her own arms. "Because we were getting a divorce. We'd agreed."

"So that's it? You get laid and sever all ties?"

She licked her lips, the little liar. Jack could

smell the fear coming off her. She liked him in the box he occupied in her life, too, and sex on the rooftop made things a little messy for Mia. A little scary.

"It seemed like the best idea."

"Right," he snapped. "Worked great, Mia." He turned to grab his sandwich and leave, but his knee got stuck under him and he lurched sideways to keep his balance.

She reached for him, but he shot her a look of such scathing anger that she backed right off.

He grabbed his sandwich and paused for a second before leaving, making sure his limbs would do as he asked without embarrassing him in front of his wife.

God, *his wife*. It sounded ridiculous.

"Look at you, you'd burn to the ground before asking anyone for help," she said.

Pain sliced through him and he flinched. His sandwich slid off the plate to floor. He was blindsided by the smell of smoke. The screams of the dying.

Mia swore and knelt at his feet to pick up his dinner. Her curls gleamed in the half-light, and he wanted to touch them. Touch her. But he was cemented in place; the desert had a hold on him that he could not break.

"I'm sorry, Jack," she murmured, putting his sandwich back on his plate. "That was a poor choice of words."

I'll say.

"How long are you staying?" she asked.

"Does it matter?"

"Maybe not to you," she said, her temper igniting in her eyes. "But I'm curious."

So was he, frankly. For the first time in his life he didn't have a plan. Or any forward momentum. He was inert and he couldn't imagine anything that would inspire movement.

"Your father said something about the board of directors having a meeting—"

He laughed, dark and gritty. "What would he know about it?"

"He saw it on the school's website," she said.

He picked floor fuzz off his sandwich. If Sandra had been here, she'd have had a fit. About the fuzz and the fact that he was going to eat the sandwich anyway.

The bread was soft under his fingers and it seemed like enough for the moment. As if holding the sandwich and talking to Mia was all he could handle right now.

"The meeting is in six weeks."

"And then?"

"Then…" He shook his head. "Then I'm not sure."

"What are you talking about?" she asked. He tried not to look at her, focusing on the hard crust of the bread, the drip of jam, because looking at her would give him another host of things he needed to deal with—desire, anger, grief and nostalgia—and the weight of it all might kill him.

His overloaded life was why he stayed in bed all day. Bed he could manage. One blank moment followed by another. No demands. Nothing more than what he could hold.

"Your job, the drill—"

"There's no more drill, Mia," he said.

"Well, not there, clearly. But you have others—"

Jack shook his head. He may be lost in his life, but he knew this. "Without Oliver there is no drill."

"But the university? Your job?"

"I'm on a leave of absence." It felt good to heave this stuff off his chest. The decisions he'd made in his hospital bed still made sense. The idea of going back to campus, to his job, made him ill.

"How long?"

"Indefinite."

"Because of your hand—"

"Because I screwed up!" he yelled and she rocked back.

Yes, you did, the voices cooed. *Yes, you really did.*

"Screwed what up?" she asked into the electrified silence.

He looked at her for a long time, seeing his reflection in her amber eyes.

Who the hell is that guy? he wondered in a panic. A stranger. A fool with a sandwich.

"Forget it, Mia. It doesn't matter."

"Yes, it does." She stepped in front of him when he tried to walk back down the hallway and he thought about pushing her out of his way. But she'd push back. It was what Mia did.

"Look at you, Jack. You're skin and bones. You lock yourself up in that room all damn day and you roam the house at night. It doesn't take a genius to see you're not sleeping. Doesn't take a genius to see that something is eating you up."

"You going to be my confessor?" he asked, his voice a wicked lick of sarcasm. Something awful was waking up inside him, a beast he couldn't contain. His hurt and anger at the way she'd left him that night in Santa Barbara, the way the events had unfolded from there, had created a two-headed monster out for blood.

"I would rather be your friend," she said.

He licked his lips, his eyes on the hallway behind her shoulder. "Not my wife?"

She laughed, the sound finding every raw spot, every vulnerable place inside him. "You never really needed one of those, Jack."

He practically threw the plate onto the dining table and stepped up to her, way closer than was comfortable. He walked until he could feel her breath on his face. The warmth of her body against the cold shell of his own.

"Why'd you run away that night, Mia?" he asked, nailing her to the ground with his eyes.

She opened her mouth, but no words came out.

His smile was wolfish. And his fingers—suddenly hungry for heat and the sensation of the living—touched her cheek. His thumb landed on the corner of her lush mouth, and she gasped.

Again, the voices, those whispers of self-destruction, chimed in. *We want her. Again. And again.*

"I know why you left," he whispered and her eyes flared. "Because you're a coward." He was close enough to kiss her, so he did, pressing his lips to hers, moving so close their chests touched and heat rippled over him.

Against her lips, he whispered, "And so am I."

He stepped away, picked up his sandwich and started to go back to his room. The medicine bottles on the dresser. The silence.

"What am I supposed to do with you?" she whispered.

"Nothing, Mia," he said, wishing, for her sake, that he had a better answer. "Not one damn thing."

MIA FELT AS THOUGH she'd just barely shut her eyes when the lowing woke her up. The deep guttural cry of a dozen cows in pain rolled over the Rocky M, right into her bedroom.

It's started, she thought, awake in a heartbeat. Elation fueled her and she pushed off her covers and grabbed fresh clothes from her dresser.

The sky was pink and gray, the clouds milky.

Her light at the end of the tunnel looked like dawn and she couldn't love it more.

In the barn, Chris was already pulling out the tattoo pliers and ear tags.

"Tim's out there," he said. "We've got one calf on the ground. Two more should be coming soon. All of them look good. Billy's on his way—he's making coffee. I figure Billy and Tim can handle the cows, Jeremiah and I can process and you can do the paperwork and float."

"Sounds good," she said. "I'll call Jeremiah."

Blue stood in his stall, his big brown eyes trained on Mia. "Not this morning, bud," she whispered, giving the horse a scratch between the eyes.

They had a landline in the tack room and

a list of frequently called numbers written on the whitewashed wall beside it. Halfway down, past Dr. Peuse, the big-game vet in town, the name Annie was scratched out and Jeremiah penciled in.

She dialed the number, wincing as she thought about the young cowboy and the early morning. But he'd agreed.

Surprisingly, the phone was answered on the first ring.

"Hello?" said a little voice. Crap. It was one of the kids.

"Hi, Eli?" She took a stab with the middle kid.

"Casey."

"Sorry, Casey." It was the baby. Wow. When had the baby grown up enough to answer the phone? At Annie's funeral he'd been a little bump in his grandpa's arms. Of course, all three boys, even Jacob, the twelve-year-old, had looked like babies that day. "Is your uncle there?"

"You bet," he said.

Mia pinched the bridge of her nose. "Could you get him?"

"You bet."

The phone clattered and in a few seconds

she heard Jeremiah's voice and Casey's excited whisper.

"Hi, this is Jeremiah."

"I'm sorry, am I waking you up?"

"No," Jeremiah grumbled, his deep voice sounding as if it were sprinkled with gravel. "Casey took care of that. Casey always takes care of that. Your calves coming?"

"Yeah," she said. "We could use you as soon as you can get here."

"No problem. I'll wake up Jacob and be over there in a half hour."

"I owe you, Jeremiah."

His laugh was weary and she again wondered how Jeremiah Stone, rodeo star, was handling the turn his life had taken after his sister's death.

"I'll remember that," he said with a laugh.

They hung up and Mia grabbed her pocket-size notebook, made sure she had the right forms and at least three pens in her shirt pocket. She pulled the beat-up black kit out from under the wobbly table in the corner and checked that she had enough syringes and vitamin E shots.

It was going to be a busy day.

THE SUN WAS HOT by ten and a furnace by noon. Sweat ran down Mia's back and across her face, but the day was going well.

Most of the newly born calves had found the teat and were nursing. There were three cows who had been in labor a long time and she was getting worried about breech calves.

"You want me to call Peuse?" Jeremiah asked, not looking up from the calf whose ear he was tagging. They stood by the open bed of the truck that had become their processing center.

"Not yet," she said, holding the calf with all of her strength. Her muscles burned from the effort.

"We're good," he muttered and set down the tattoo pliers. Together they lifted the calf to the ground, where he stood, wobbled and lowed for his mama.

Mama lowed back and the calf, on shaky newborn legs, staggered to the left of the truck.

"Tim!" she heard Chris yell, his voice laced with panic. She turned away from the mama and calf reunion and searched the far side of the pasture for any sign of her guys.

"Tim, watch it! She's on her feet! Tim—"

Mia and Jeremiah shared a quick look and then took off at a run for the small hill and copse of trees in the corner of the field.

Chris and Tim met them at the top of hill. Tim, the almost always silent cowboy, was swearing like a sailor and holding his hand wrapped in a shirt that was quickly turning red.

"It's not that bad," he said quickly, when he saw Mia's face.

She glanced up at Chris who shook his head. "Two fingers are broken and he should get stitches."

"What the hell happened?" she asked, pushing her hat back on her head.

"He got between the calf and the dam," Chris said.

"You're kidding me," she moaned. Such a beginner's mistake.

"I think my five-year-old knows better," Jeremiah said with a wicked twinkle in his blue eyes.

"This isn't funny!" she yelled and all the men straightened. "We're not even a quarter of the way through the herd. And I can't spare one man, much less two, so you can get chauffeured into town to get looked at."

"I can stitch him up," Jeremiah said. He lifted his hat and ran his fingers through sweaty black curls.

"Really?" she asked.

"I did it all the time on the circuit."

Those rodeo guys were a tough bunch.

"What about the fingers?" she asked.

"Tape 'em," Tim said, looking contrite and pained. "I'll be fine."

"No," Chris said. "You'll be one-handed, at best."

One-handed. One-handed, when she was three men short.

"Do what you can," she said and watched as Tim and Jeremiah walked back toward the barn.

In the distance, the house sat in the shadows of the granite cliff behind it. A house with two men in it.

She tried to take a calming breath to divert the sudden river of purpose that had welled up in her. But there was no diverting it. She was short men and the house was lousy with them.

Walter, she knew, even with the medicine, would be no good out here.

But Jack was another matter.

He'd taken off that cast. Wasn't walking with a cane.

Just thinking his name ignited a brush fire in her brain.

Jack, who'd seen and worked a dozen calving seasons.

Jack, who'd called her a coward last night and then hid in his room like a child. Jack, whose dark eyes and mercurial animosity had kept her awake tossing and turning most of the night, tormented by anger and a very unwanted lust.

She'd never asked for a damn thing, not once in five years of marriage.

And she'd been proud of that.

But now it was going to change.

CHAPTER SEVEN

THE DOOR OPENED easily under her fist and Jack, lying on his bed, sat up. Mia's eyes raked his bare chest, the lean strong muscles.

She worried briefly about his injuries, but she could get him to process with Jeremiah. He could still work a pencil and a tagging gun.

"Mia?" he asked, nonplussed, his lips curved in a strange little smile and she realized she was still staring at his chest.

She flung open the door to his closet, but it was empty. So were the drawers in his dresser.

"You looking for something?" he asked.

The duffel bag beside his bed was overflowing with T-shirts and jeans. She picked up one of each and threw them at him.

"Get dressed," she said.

"What are you doing, Mia?" He sighed. "I told you I just wanted to be—"

"I'm drowning!" she snapped, her hands in fists at her side because she wanted to grab him and shake him. She didn't want to need him. She didn't want to beg him for help, but her back was so far against the wall she was about to become wallpaper.

"I'm three men short, Tim's hurt and we're not even a quarter through the herd."

Jack glanced out the bare window. At the big blue sky outside. She couldn't read his still face, couldn't see her old friend in those familiar features, the man who would have been the first guy out the door this morning to help her.

Mia pulled the words that didn't want to see the light of day out from the very back of her throat. "I need you, Jack," she said through her teeth. "Five years of marriage and I never asked you for—"

He held up his hand. "You don't have to beg," he said and shoved an arm through his shirt. "Give me a minute."

JACK STUMBLED OUT into the pasture like one of the calves. New and unsure. The sun was bright, the smells powerful. It was an assault on every sense he'd been wrapping in gauze for the past few weeks.

"Jack?" Chris, the lean, tough foreman who'd been working here since Jack was a kid, stepped up to his left and Jack tried not to flinch in surprise. Christ, he was jumpy.

Back inside! the voices cried. *Back to bed!*

"Hey, Chris," he said, trying to fake a smile.

"I'd shake but—" Chris held up his hands, swathed in gloves, covered in blood.

Jack nodded. "Deferred shake," he said with a laugh.

"On account of your hand and knee, we're going to put you up on the truck—"

"My hand is fine," he said, not entirely sure why. But now that he was here, he wasn't blind to the work. He remembered how tired Mia had looked last night, passed out in the chair, and guilt hit hard. A week he'd been hiding in that bedroom, more a coward than he thought. "So's my knee."

Chris blinked, those cagey blue eyes missing nothing. "Okay, then," he said. "You can be with Billy down at the chute. We're waiting for Peuse to handle a couple of difficult births."

Jack nodded. He wanted to ask where Mia was, but he bit back the question.

He approached the chute and a young hand—Billy, he supposed—handed him tattoo pliers and ear tags. "Right ear for bulls, left for—"

For a second the hand's voice was drowned out by his father's telling him the exact same thing when he was nine years old, helping out on his first calving.

"Heifers. I remember," Jack said. And he did. Eighteen years of his life surrounded by cattle. He'd forgotten the rituals, but they surfaced as soon as he stepped into the chute. They weren't unwelcome, not like the memories of his mother. His father. Those he kept locked away, never to resurface. But he'd always liked the work. Liked that it was an entire world in and of itself, while at the same time a part of a cumulative whole. It felt good to turn off his brain and use his body.

His muscles, asleep and stiff, woke up to

the exertion and within a few minutes, he was sweating and swearing with Billy.

Within a few hours, the voices were silent.

PEUSE CAME AND WENT, treating two calves with scours, and by nightfall, a good two-thirds of the calves had been born. The remaining third looked good to go in the next few days, at a far more reasonable pace. Jack was covered head to toe in the realities of calving.

"You stink, man," Billy said. The good-natured cowboy had been cracking jokes all day, and the pull of camaraderie was painful.

Because Oliver, his comrade, the great jokester, the man Jack'd worked beside more hours than he could count, was dead. Blown into so many pieces there was nothing left to bury.

Jack didn't want to joke. To shoot the shit. Not with anyone but his old friend.

He wanted to work himself into stillness. Quiet.

So, it was easier to resist Billy's efforts

at chumminess. To hold himself distant and aloof.

"Go on and take a shower," Jack told Billy. The role of boss had never been a tough one for him. "Get some food."

"I better check on Mia. She hasn't had a break all day."

"She works hard," Jack said. The loyalty she inspired in her men was significant. And he was proud of her.

"There's more work than people. She does her share and then some."

Jack turned to Billy as a question that had bothered him since he first returned to the ranch came back around. "Where are all the seasonal guys?" he asked. "Every spring we'd hire a few extra guys. Why hasn't Mia?"

Billy shrugged. "You'll have to ask her, but I'm pretty sure there ain't any money to do it."

"Come on," Jack scoffed. "No money for spring cowboys?"

Billy nodded. "Your old man did a number on this place—"

Jack jerked. "Dad?"

Billy waved his hands. "This conversation is way above my pay grade," he said. "You want to ask those kinds of questions, better talk to Mia."

Jack nodded. "Go on in," he said. "I'll check on her." Billy didn't need the offer a third time. He made his way around the chute and headed toward the bunkhouse.

Chris and Tim had already gone to get food put together, but he hadn't seen Mia in the past few hours.

The sky was indigo against the black mountains. Soon it would be fully dark, the sliver of a moon not much illumination, and he couldn't leave her out here to finish whatever work was left.

He headed toward the far corner of the pasture, toward the hill and the trees where most of the cows seemed to go once they knew birth was close.

Cresting the hill, he saw Mia sitting cross-legged on the ground, feeding a calf from a bottle, while the dam licked the baby.

A man crouched beside her and as Jack watched, the stranger cupped her shoulder, smiled into her face. Intimately. Mia's laugh, weary and throaty, echoed over the small valley. The man said something in Spanish and she responded in kind.

Jealousy made a sudden, angry puncture wound in his chest. *I can speak Spanish,* he thought, sullen and childish.

"Mia," he said, as he approached. She turned, looking at him over her shoulder. The cowboy stood up and tipped back his hat.

"Hi, Jack," he said, a slow-burning smile crossing his familiar face. "Been a while."

It took a second but soon the dots connected in his head. "Jeremiah Stone," he said with a laugh. Their closest neighbor. He and Jeremiah had gone to school together until Jeremiah dropped out of high school to be a rodeo stud. They hadn't had a whole lot in common—some summer baseball games, a mutual crush on Helen Jones. They had been two different kinds of boys.

As soon as Jeremiah got to his feet, as a baby, he'd run wild.

But Jack had always liked the guy.

"How are you?" Jack asked, reaching out to shake his old friend's hand.

"Not bad," Jeremiah said.

"You visiting Annie?" he asked, remembering Jeremiah's redheaded spitfire of an older sister.

Jeremiah's eyes went dark and Mia ducked her head, coughing into her sleeve.

"Annie died," Jeremiah said, his voice tight. "Cancer."

"When?" Jack asked, grief for his old friend blowing through him.

"A few months ago. I've taken over the ranch."

"Where's Gibson?" he asked, referring to Annie's husband.

"He died in a car accident three years back," Jeremiah said.

Jeremiah's face was shuttered and Jack got the firm impression that he didn't want to answer any other questions.

And there was nothing Jack understood better.

"I'm sorry," Jack said. "She was a good woman."

Jeremiah nodded, his jaw hard.

"Go on home," Mia said, breaking the unbearable tension of the moment. "And thank you so much."

"No problem," Jeremiah said. He glanced up at Jack. "You can repay me by fixing that pump up in the high pasture."

"It's broken again?" she asked, her voice so weary it practically fell asleep on her lips.

Jeremiah nodded, his blue eyes watching Jack. "Good thing the water man is back," he said. He slapped Jack's shoulder and tipped his hat again. "'Night, folks."

Jeremiah walked away, leaving Jack and Mia alone among the nursing cows. He watched Mia stroke the soft ear of the calf beside her. Her fingers looked so small, so delicate.

"I didn't know about his sister," he whispered. "Or Gibson."

"I emailed you when it happened. Both times," she said and he winced. Probably only one of a million things that hadn't registered on the plane of his life.

He thought of Jeremiah, the handsome cowboy, the charm that had cut through the female population of Wassau Public School like a blade through butter. The bad-boy rodeo star with a wicked grin had been a potent teenager and seemed to be just as potent a man.

"Is Jeremiah why you want a divorce?"

She gaped at him for a moment before

bursting into laughter, startling the calf in her lap.

"Shhh," she cooed, coaxing the animal's mouth back to the bottle.

"Is he?"

"No, Jack. He isn't why I want a divorce. He's taken over Stone's Hollow and his sister's three boys. He barely has time to sleep, much less seduce the neighbors."

Three boys. He looked back at the cowboy getting into his truck in the wide gravel lot beside the barn. The idea of Jeremiah raising kids didn't seem to fit, but then not much did these days.

Jack sat down in the grass beside Mia, his body so grateful for the rest it nearly cheered.

"How's the calf?" he asked, pointing to the baby still sucking on the bottle.

"Calf is fine, big as all get-out, but Mom isn't producing any colostrum yet."

"You give her some extra feed?"

She nodded and the silence stretched out.

"Thanks for your help today," she said, not looking at him, while he couldn't seem to take his eyes off her.

"You're working too hard," he said.

"Well, you know, 'tis the season."

"You need a few extra hands around here, Mia," he said.

"You don't have to tell me."

"Billy said something about there not being enough money to hire anyone."

Mia's head turned so fast her ponytail whipped the side of his face. "Billy's a gossip."

"Most cowboys are," he said. "Is it true?"

She pulled the drained bottle from the calf's mouth and got to her feet.

"You suddenly care about this ranch?"

"No."

"Then stop asking—"

"I care about you, Mia. I always have."

"Well, you have a pretty crappy way of showing it, Jack!" she snapped. "You show up here and lock yourself in your room." She crouched and gathered her stuff, the gritty gloves, the case for vitamin E shots, mumbling under her breath. "You won't answer my questions. I have to force you—"

He put a hand over hers and she stilled. He

shouldn't have kissed her last night. It was stupid. Made things muddy between them.

"I'm sorry," he said, watching her.

"For what?" She lifted her face and met his eyes. The electrical current of their connection buzzed through him.

"For showing up the way I did." Her forthright gaze was too much and he looked away. He had a lot to apologize for. "For treating you the way I did the other night. I've been..." God, what could he say?

"A mess?"

He smiled. "Sure, we'll go with a mess."

"You have every right, Jack. What you've been through—"

"Well, I didn't need to take it out on you. I'm sorry about last night."

Perhaps it was a trick of the fading light, but it looked as if Mia was blushing and he wondered if she'd gone to bed thinking of his fingers on her face. Her lips.

A hot wave of desire rolled over him and he was suddenly desperate for the taste of her again, for a taste of life before the bombing.

"I still want a divorce," she said, and he

felt like a fool, sitting there with half an erection.

"Fine," he said, pushing himself to his feet. "I won't stop you."

She nodded once, looking for a moment as if she had something else to say, but in the end she just turned on her heel, took three steps and stopped again.

He would have smiled if he was still that kind of guy.

"I have to ask," she said, bowing her head. Her neck, white in the dusk, seemed so vulnerable, so achingly appealing he wanted to press a hundred kisses to her soft skin. Her heartbeat.

"Oliver?" she asked, and he flinched, all tender thoughts obliterated. He didn't say anything, couldn't say anything. She turned, her eyes damp.

"What about him?" he asked, unable to push a woman with so much grief in her eyes, grief he understood far too well, away.

"Was he in pain…before he died?" she whispered. "Was he scared?"

Oh, Mia, he thought, her sorrow tearing through him.

He shook his head, wondering how to tell

her that all they found of Oliver after the bombing was a shoe and his flask.

"It was fast," he whispered and she sighed in relief.

Before he knew it, she was in front of him, wrapping her strong arms around his waist, pulling them together. Her hands were warm and wide on his back.

"I'm so sorry," she whispered. "You must miss him so much."

The contact was distracting, like very loud static. He couldn't think past all the noise his body was making. But slowly the comfort of her touch seeped into him, shoving aside his grief and guilt, touching him in those cold dark places that he didn't think would ever feel warmth again.

"I do," he breathed. And pulled her against him as if his life depended on it.

CHAPTER EIGHT

IT TOOK FOUR DAYS for the cows of the Rocky M to finish the calving. Mia assigned the guys to shifts and Jack was surprised to be happy about working at night alongside Chris. Despite his exhaustion, the nightmares were frequent and harrowing and he slept better during the day, or maybe not as deeply as at night.

And Chris was good company. He'd been a young hand when Jack was growing up and if he knew what was going on in the house, he didn't say anything.

Like the other guys, Jack worked and ate and slept without any regard to a clock. He didn't think. The voices were silent, the pills no longer a magnetic threat on his bedside table.

Mia didn't seem to sleep, or if she did he didn't see it. Every time he turned around she was there with the tattoo pliers, or talking to Dr. Peuse about the three calves who had been weakened by diarrhea.

On the third day he walked into the tack room and found her snoring on a wooden upright chair.

"Don't wake her," Chris said over his shoulder.

"You're kidding," Jack said.

Chris shook his head. "You wake her and she'll start working again. This way she'll get a little sleep."

"And a sore neck."

Chris shrugged, but Jack saw the man's concern in his blue eyes.

"This is crazy," Jack said.

"This is the Rocky M." Chris headed out through the barn toward the calving pasture.

Mia's head bobbed forward onto her chest; she started, but didn't wake.

And she calls me stubborn, he thought.

He couldn't leave her like that. But at the same time, Chris was right, which meant he just had to be sure Mia didn't wake up. Jack bent beside her, sliding one hand behind her back, the other under her knees.

Close up, he realized she smelled as bad

as the rest of them and for some reason, that was endearing. He wanted to peel off her filthy clothes and put her in a bath. Clean her. Feed her. Put her to bed for a week.

Want and regret clashed in his chest. He was sure no one had ever done that for her before. She was thirty years old and no man had ever taken care of her, pampered her. If he'd been a real husband, it would have been his right.

His privilege.

He stood, lifting her easily in his arms. His skin, his whole body woke up at the contact.

But then so did she.

He stopped, embarrassed and slightly angry that she was so stubborn he had to resort to these cheesy tactics just to get her to bed.

"What the hell are you doing?" she asked.

"You fell asleep in the chair." He sounded guilty to his own ears, like a teenager caught copping a feel. He quickly put her on her feet, trying not to notice the way her body leaned into his. Warm and lush, every curve a reminder that she was his wife and he'd been celibate a long, long time.

"And you couldn't just wake me up?"

"I wanted you to sleep."

"Then you should have left me alone," she said. "I was sleeping fine."

"That's what Chris said."

"What the hell, Jack? Did you bring everyone through to vote?"

"We're just worried about you."

"I'm fine!"

"Sure you are," he snapped back. "Because everyone who's fine falls asleep in a drafty barn in an upright chair. For crying out loud, Mia, go to bed before you fall over."

"It's none of your business, Jack."

"I am still your husband—"

She stepped back, blinked and then howled with laughter. He burned at the sound. He was just trying to help. Just trying to make sure she didn't collapse under the weight of this damn ranch.

"Oh, come on, Jack, don't be mad. I'm fine. Honestly, I feel better." She smiled. "We'll all sleep when the week is out."

She stepped away, heading for the stables, back to the endless work, but then she stopped. Paused in the doorway.

Hesitant. Careful. Shy, almost. He saw that shy girl she'd been in the woman of steel she'd become.

"Thanks," she said.

And all he could do was nod.

WALTER MANAGED to be useful by pulling casserole after casserole out of the freezer for the guys. Jack ate chicken pot pie for breakfast, lunch and dinner and had no complaints. The old man made coffee so strong it could strip paint, and he made lots of it.

The laundry situation got so dire that Jack found Billy dressed in plaid Bermuda shorts, of all things, spraying a hose at five pairs of manure- and mud-crusted jeans that he'd thrown over the horse paddock's fence.

"I'm outta jeans," Billy said.

"You look like a cowboy surfer," Jack said.

"You're not much better, corporate cowboy," Billy pointed out, flicking the hose at him.

Jack howled and leaped out of the way, but he wasn't fast enough to keep his last pair of pants—khaki chinos—dry. "Watch it, man. I'm out of jeans, too," he said, laughing.

He could only avoid the camaraderie among men working too hard for so long. And after a while, he didn't even want to. It felt good to have friends again. To laugh again.

"Well, bring me your pants and we'll hose 'em off before throwing them in the machine."

Jack shook his head. "What about the housekeeper?" he asked. It was a rare cowboy who did his own laundry.

"Gloria'll be in tomorrow," Billy said. "But I'm desperate now."

Jack was, too, and he went off to gather up the stinky pile of denim in the corner of his room.

When the last cow had given birth and the last calf was tagged at twilight on the fourth day, everyone, Jack included, fell into bed and slept for twelve hours.

But at dawn, Jack woke with a start, staring up at the white ceiling from the sagging mattress on his single bed. He knew exactly what needed to be done. It was so obvious, he couldn't believe that Mia hadn't thought of it herself. Although, considering how tired she was, how the nonstop work must seem like a track she couldn't get off, it wasn't all that surprising.

He stepped into the kitchen just after sunrise, surprised to find both Mia and Walter already sitting at the table. A pot of coffee was set between them and, oddly, what looked like a bag of sliced ham.

"Morning," he said. Both Walter and Mia spun to face him. He didn't even glance at his father, refusing to see the hope on that face like an open wound.

That hope was ridiculous after all his father had done. Or not done, as was more often the case.

"Morning, Jack," Mia said. "Ham?" She lifted the bag toward him.

He shook his head, a little grossed out.

"Suit yourself," she said and tossed a piece in her mouth.

See, he thought, she didn't have the energy or inclination to get herself a proper breakfast. Something needed to be done and if she couldn't see to it to do it herself, he would help.

"You guys didn't replace Sandra with a

full-time housekeeper?" he asked. Having a cook and housekeeper at the ranch was a pretty integral part of the life. Cowboys had been known to leave jobs on account of crappy food.

Walter's expression turned defensive. "Gloria comes in—"

"Part-time, I know. You need someone more than that."

"Gloria does all right by us." His father's familiar voice hit Jack's body like a barrage of dirt and small stones. It stung and he wanted to walk away, but he'd spent enough time ignoring the tailspin the ranch was in.

"What about the men?" Jack asked. "Chris and Billy and Tim, who cooks for them?"

"They manage on their own for breakfast and lunch. Dinner, Mia heats up something that Gloria puts in the freezer. We all eat in here, like we used to." Dad was answering his questions like a star pupil. Was, in fact, talking to him more at this moment than he had for the last two years Jack had lived in this house.

It made Jack want to smash things.

"Why all the questions, Jack?" Mia asked, her eyes narrowed.

"I'm just trying to figure out what's going on around here."

"Work," she said. "Like always."

"Right. Work with half the staff you need, and no housekeeper. No cook." Jack pointed down at her breakfast. "After four eighteen-hour days, you're eating ham out of a bag, Mia."

Mia pushed the bag away. "What's your point?"

Finally, he turned and faced his father. Walter's face was covered with nicks and little bandages as if a raccoon had shaved his face for him. "Where's the money?" he asked his dad. "Your savings, the emergency accounts?"

"It was a bad winter," Mia interrupted as if trying to deflect his attention away from his dad.

"There have been other bad winters," he said, not looking away from his father's rheumy gray eyes.

"Jack—"

"I am talking to my father," Jack snapped.

"What do you want me to say?" Walter asked. "We're broke. Your mom took a chunk in the divorce."

"Mom, of course," he muttered.

"Your dad got sick," Mia said. "The medication is expensive and a lot of it isn't covered by insurance. There were some tax problems—"

"What kind of tax problems?" Jack asked.

"The kind that cost money," Mia said wearily.

"How much?" Jack asked, through thin lips.

"Enough—"

"How much!"

"Fifty thousand dollars. But with the calves—"

"Holy shit, Dad. What happened?"

"I screwed up," Walter said. "After you left and your mom and I divorced, I...screwed up."

"Were you drinking again?" Jack asked, and Walter nodded, lifting his trembling hands toward the coffee cup in front of him. "Are you still?"

Walter said nothing and Mia's sad sigh was all the answer Jack needed.

"All right," he said. "That, in a way, makes things easier. Dad, I know you're not going to agree with this, but you've pretty much screwed yourself out of the ability to make this decision."

"What kind of decision?"

"I'm going to sell the ranch."

MIA LAUGHED. She couldn't help it. The laughter just sputtered out of her.

"You're kidding, right?" she asked, picking up the bag of ham again.

"No, Mia, I'm not," Jack said. She could tell by his face he wasn't joking.

A thousand bees invaded Mia's head, spread throughout her body, making it impossible to think. To breathe. This ranch was her home. Her life. Jack was talking about selling her life, as if it was nothing.

And he could do it.

She had no legal rights to any of what she'd built here. If he really wanted to do this, she had no say.

The injustice, the ridiculousness of it, burned through the numbness.

"You're getting ahead of yourself, Jack," Walter said, his voice laced with the old steel. "I'm not dead yet."

"No," Jack agreed, looking cold and

removed. "But it won't be too hard to prove that you're unfit to make the decision. You're drinking. You're sick and my guess is you're not taking your meds—"

"I am," he insisted.

Mia started to shake her head. Were they nuts? Was Jack…nuts?

Anger churned in her belly. She would fight him. She would fight him with everything she had.

"In order to clear whatever debt you have and make sure that you're cared for as you get sicker—and that Mia has a chance at a life she deserves—you need to get rid of this place."

"A life I deserve?" Mia stood, the legs of the chair screeching against the floor as she backed up. "What the hell would you know about it, Jack?"

"I know this place is going to wear you down to nothing," he said. "Between the work, paying off the debt and taking care of an old drunk—"

Walter flinched at the word; Jack saw it but didn't say anything. Clearly he didn't care.

"We're not selling the ranch," she said. "As your wife, I have some say in this."

"We're getting a divorce, remember? You don't get a vote."

She reeled back as if he'd slapped her. He wouldn't sink so low. Or maybe he would. She didn't know anymore.

"You can't do this, Jack," she snapped. "You can't just swoop in here—"

"I'm not trying to be malicious," he said.

"Let me finish my sentence!" she yelled, banging her hand on the table. That got his attention. "You're not listening to us. You can't swoop in here and sell this ranch. You don't have the right to make that decision."

She wanted to slap that baffled look right off his face. "Someone has to, and you two sure as hell aren't doing it."

Mia shook her head, so angry and hurt she trembled. Every argument she needed to make sputtered and died under the weight of her anger.

Between the work and the lack of sleep, the past week had worn her out, and she couldn't put together a string of coherent words. She needed a second to get her thoughts together, to be able to have a conversation that wouldn't end with her smacking him.

Leaving her cup and the ham behind, she grabbed her hat and took off for the barn.

WALTER STARED at his son, wondering what kind of devil lived in that boy's head.

"What the hell is wrong with you?" Walter asked.

"I'm just trying to do what's right," Jack whispered.

"I don't think Mia's going to see it that way," Walter said.

Jack turned to face him, and Walter tried not to shrink under his damning gaze. He'd done wrong by his son a thousand times and it wasn't anything he was proud of.

"You should be ashamed of yourself," Jack said.

"I am," he said and that seemed to bring Jack up short. The apologies Walter had saved up over the years, the regrets he'd carried in his palms like river stones, were burdens he rushed to unload. He reached for his son. "I should have protected you. I should have seen—"

"Not me," Jack snapped. "Her!" He pointed out the window to where Mia was making her way across the grass toward the barn.

One of the dogs circled her, no doubt smelling the ham on her fingers.

"If you want to help me," Jack said, "if you want to make things right between us, then help me convince her to sell the ranch. Help me get her free of this place."

Free of this place? Walter shook his head, so sad that his only son, his flesh and blood, saw the ranch that way.

Walter had been blindsided when Jack and Mia got married five years ago. He'd always known they were close…but marriage? But Walter had stopped understanding his son by the time Jack had become a teenager.

As the years went by and Walter finally caught on that Jack and Mia's relationship was a marriage in name only, he'd kept his mouth shut.

He'd watched Mia walk out that door a few times a year to meet Jack someplace, with her eyes alight like a girl's on a first date.

And she always came back hollowed out.

As hollowed as Jack was now, watching Mia cross the long yard to the barn.

Stupid kids, Walter thought, *wasting so much time*. They didn't know how precious time was, how it could run in the other direction, a train they had no chance of catching.

Two weeks ago, Walter had believed that his son's being back at the ranch was a chance to make the mistakes of his past right.

But now, standing amid the wreckage of his son's marriage, Walter wondered if it was a chance for Jack to correct his own mistakes.

Walter hoped so. For the girl out in that barn who worked so hard and loved so much. And for Jack…who deserved a shot at being happy. At being loved.

Walter stood, arranging his shaky, weak limbs beneath his weight. He'd shrunk since getting sick, but he was still a big man and when he stood up straight, Jack blinked.

"You got it wrong, boy," he said. "You want to help her, drop this idea of selling the ranch."

"That's you talking—" Jack began. Walter cut him off with a shake of his head.

"Go out there and talk to her," he said. "Listen to her. She'll tell you."

Walter was glad he'd gotten rid of the walker in favor of the cane. It made a better exit.

JACK FOUND HER out in the barn, the remaining calving supplies spread out across the tack room table.

Good God, the woman was doing inventory.

"Mia," he said.

Mia's back stiffened and her anger was so palpable the dog at her feet whined.

"Mia," Jack said to the back of her head. "Can I talk to you?"

"I'm busy," she muttered.

"Mia—"

"Fine." She turned, her face so composed she looked like someone else. Someone older and colder. He was off balance around this version of her. Sun hit dust motes in the air, turning them to glitter that matched the gold in her eyes.

"I'm not trying to piss you off," he said.

"Let me guess. You're trying to help."

"Yes," he said. "Why is that a bad thing?"

"Because selling the ranch isn't going to *help,* Jack." She was looking at him as if he was the fool for not realizing this. And he honestly didn't understand why she couldn't see it his way.

"You're bleeding money."

"Not anymore. We had a good calving season and once we go to market, I can pay the taxes."

"But you're shorthanded. You need at least three more guys in the barn, not to mention a live-in housekeeper. Dad is drinking—"

"Your dad always drank."

"Yeah, but now he's sick. And Parkinson's, no matter what, only gets worse, Mia. Not better."

"But if he keeps taking his meds he could have years before I need to worry about what to do with him."

"And then what?"

"And then I'll think of something. Or maybe, just maybe, you'll step up and do something. As his son."

The shot registered down deep, but he pushed it aside. He was good at that. All the things in front of him were organized, clear. His work. His job. Even his marriage. All neatly labeled and properly shelved.

But all those emotions he pushed to the side, the memories of his parents and his past that he refused to deal with, were a jumbled mess on the outskirts of his life. And they were beginning to cloud his vision.

"Mia, that's no way to plan."

"I don't have any other answer, Jack. Because I am *not* selling this ranch."

"What about the divorce?" He waited for her answer, unsure of when he'd started to care about what that answer might be.

She chewed her lip. "Forget it."

He laughed, his pride prickling. "You'll stay married to me in order to keep this place?"

"It's my home!" she declared, her eyes catching fire. "And I get that you don't understand how I feel—"

"Of course I do," he snapped back. "It's why I married you in the first place. So you could keep your home. So you could have the life you told me you always wanted. But this isn't that life."

"You don't get to decide that, Jack! You don't get to waltz back in here and make these sweeping decisions on my behalf."

"I'm not."

"Oh, Jack, you don't even see it. That's what you do. You walk into a world, change it and then leave before the dust settles. You don't stick around to see what you've done."

He blinked and took a step back. Another. His stomach ached, the truth like stones rattling around inside him.

"Are you talking about Africa?" he asked. She'd torn the blinders from his eyes, and the world she'd revealed was different than the one he knew.

He wasn't always the hero. Africa was complicated and he treated his work there like it was simple. A problem to solve.

That was how he treated everything. Because it was simpler.

She paused, her lips parted. "Maybe," she said. "I don't know. I just know what you did to me five years ago."

"Five years ago you needed me. Just like you need me now. This isn't emotional, Mia. It's reality."

She stepped up close, so close he smelled the coffee on her breath. "You want the reality?" The word slashed and burned between them, changing everything, and the hair on the back of his neck stood on end. "I didn't need you then, Jack. And I don't need you now."

"What are you talking about?"

"Five years ago, I had a job offer from

Annie Stone. She needed a foreman and I could have just moved over there—"

"But your mom? Lucy?"

"They'd already decided to move to Los Angeles. Mom wanted to go, wanted to leave the drama of this ranch behind. Start someplace fresh."

Jack tried to add it all up but things still didn't make sense.

Nothing made sense.

"Then why did you marry me?"

MIA COULDN'T RUN from this question. Had in fact driven them to this point. And she found, facing down this truth, that she wanted to get rid of this burden. This load she'd carried for so long, all by herself.

She was so tired. Tired of carrying it. Tired of pretending.

Her body went still. Her mind quieted.

This would end everything. He'd leave, she had no doubt. She'd file for the divorce and he'd sign. They'd probably never see each other again and that hurt. It hurt so much she pushed the thought away.

But Jack wasn't equipped to deal with the truth, even though he stood there talking about emotion and reality as if he had any idea what her life was really like.

She breathed the smells of the barn, the straw and feed. The horses. She'd put down roots here, roots that went all the way to the bedrock of the mountains behind her and Jack. What he thought, or what she felt about him, couldn't change that.

This was going to sting, no doubt about it, but in the end she'd be okay. Because she had these roots.

"I married you because I loved you," she said carefully. It was as if a weight, heavy and tiresome, fell from her tongue, into a silence so deep it made her dizzy.

It took a moment for her words to register but when they did Jack's jaw dropped.

She would've laughed if it hadn't hurt so badly. "I've loved you my whole life and when you said you'd marry me I said yes because I wanted to be your wife."

"Mia," he breathed, and stupidly, she couldn't move. Despite all her brave talk, she was scared. She was hopeful.

A girl standing in front of the boy she loved, with her heart shivering in the open air.

Idiot, she scolded herself, *don't do this. Don't care.*

But she couldn't help it.

Slowly, almost imperceptibly, he started to shake his head.

Oh. Oh, God. Her heart fell into pieces.

She sucked in a quick breath as if she'd been punched in the stomach, and with the breath came all the pain she knew would come with telling him how she felt. She'd kept her feelings a secret for a reason.

He didn't love her. She'd always known it and it still hurt.

Embarrassment swamped her, followed by an agony so big she had to brace herself against the stall or fall to her knees in front of him.

"Mia." He reached for her, the jackass, and she stepped away, nearly hissing in warning, a wounded animal ready to strike out. "I had no idea," he whispered.

"I know." Tears, stupid tears burned behind her eyes and she curled her hands into fists, digging her ragged nails into her palms. She'd told the truth and now she needed to work through this vast ocean of hurt. Needed to get to the other side and move on with her life.

It wasn't Jack's fault he didn't love her.

"I was always just…little Mia to you and that's okay, Jack. And I knew going in what this marriage would be like. I knew you'd be gone most of the time and that, in time, you'd probably—" She stopped, swallowed. Her pride sticking in her throat. "Find someone else."

"I didn't," he said quickly. "I mean, I never cheated."

"I know," she said. Likely because he forgot to, or got too busy looking at charts and digging holes to notice the women falling at his feet.

Just as he'd been too busy growing up and away to notice her.

"What was Santa Barbara?" he asked.

"It was goodbye." She shrugged. "You were right the other night. I was a coward. I ran because…because it hurt to finally have you just when I'd decided to let you go. And I'm sorry I didn't answer your emails. And I'm sorry I wasn't there when you needed me after the attack. I just never thought…I never thought you would."

The silence pounded against her ears as if she'd gone too deep underwater and she realized, in an instant, that she couldn't stand here anymore, watching him watch her.

She backed away. "If you want to help me—and I know you do, Jack, I've never doubted that—but if you really want to help, stop talking about selling the ranch and leave. Go back to your life. Let me have mine."

CHAPTER NINE

THE WALLS OF HIS ROOM were stifling. Suffocating. Jack walked through the rest of the house, unchanged since his mother had lived here, and he couldn't quite handle that, either. So he grabbed the keys for Mia's finicky pickup truck and then ransacked the mudroom for some tools.

"Where are you headed?" his father asked, standing in the doorway to the living room.

Go back to your life. Mia's words echoed in his mind.

"Good question, Dad," he said and left.

He remembered the well in the high pasture. He'd put it together himself as part of an advanced earth science class in high school. Frankly, he was surprised the thing still worked.

Within minutes of taking the mechanism apart, he saw that Mia had been keeping the pump together with a wing and a prayer and probably a fortune in gasket replacements. He laid the parts out on the back of the truck and did his best to clean them. The work was familiar. Comforting. Like the exertion of the past few days.

His hands got busy and his mind went right back to Mia.

I've loved you my whole life.

Had he been blind? Or was she that good at hiding her feelings? He played over every encounter in the past five years, pulling apart his memories for a clue. A sign. And maybe, in hindsight there were some, but they were practically in code.

How he must have hurt her. Over and over again. The Los Angeles trip. He remembered her sitting in that lawyer's office, listening to him talk about wills and trust funds, all the precautions Jack was taking in case he died.

And she'd sat there like a statue. Blinking into the sunlight coming in the window. Her hands clenched in her lap.

And that night, in that terrible hotel, how shy she'd been coming out of the bathroom. How quiet. So un-Mia-like. He'd barely registered it, preoccupied with the year ahead, his final preparations.

Regret choked him. Regret that he'd been so blind, so cavalier with her. And for a second he couldn't stand his own skin.

He thought about that night in Santa Barbara, the frantic way she'd made love. And how she'd left, run away while he gloated to himself in the bathroom.

I'm sorry, Mia. I'm such an ass.

He started shaving down the threading on the pump, solving the gasket problem once and for all. Wishing he could solve the problem of his life as easily.

How was it possible she loved him? he wondered. Though he had to admit her parents, Sandra and A.J., had been good role models in that department. Wildly unlike his own. Their marriage had been solid, a loving one until A.J.'s death five and a half years ago. After which, Victoria went all the way off her rocker and tried to kick Mia's family off the ranch.

But at what point had he earned Mia's love? Childhood, he supposed, those rooftop trips. He'd seen the hero worship. Hell, everyone had seen that. He'd just never been aware that it had turned into something else.

He sifted through his feelings, taking each one out to examine it, testing its weight and strength. Affection and lust he had in spades. Concern. Respect. Was it an equation? If he added up all those things, would the end result be love?

He didn't think so.

Love was something else, not that he was entirely sure what it was, but it had to be something specific. Singular. An entity in and of itself.

And he would know it if he felt it. Wouldn't he? It shouldn't be a question. Love should be a fact.

And the fact was…he didn't love Mia.

And if he couldn't love Mia, maybe he just couldn't love at all.

Go back to your life. Let me have mine.

He didn't have a life to go back to. Well, not much of one.

But he owed the university some answers. That board meeting was in three weeks.

So, he'd go back to San Luis Obispo and then…what?

He had money.

He brushed away a fly and looked up at the high pasture. The alpine flowers were coming up, small patches of yellow and white interrupting the carpet of vibrant green.

There weren't many places prettier than this, and he'd seen plenty of beauty in the world. If Mia was dead set on spending the rest of her life here, he would just have to understand that.

He had enough money to handle the Rocky M's tax problems. He would do that for her and he'd put some money aside for his father, so that when the time came, they could get a nurse.

The old man wouldn't go to a nursing home. He'd die first.

He thought of the hope on Walter's face, the very palpable desire to make amends for his past. And Jack didn't know how to tell him that no amends could be made.

The past was dead. Buried.

He needed it to be that way.

He thought of the steel in Mia's eyes, the pain. The pain he inflicted on her just by being here.

Mia was right. He needed to leave. Because he was the past for her, and she needed to move on.

BY THE AFTERNOON, Mia's head was floating someplace above her body and she wasn't sure if it was relief from finally unloading her feelings, pain from being rejected or just extreme weariness.

Either way, she had to trust that one more cup of coffee would fix that little problem.

She wasn't sure what would help the throbbing ache in her chest.

Time, maybe. Having Jack gone, probably. But she knew in her gut it was going to hurt a whole lot worse before it ever got better.

"You know," Chris said, coming up behind her in the barn, where she was saddling Blue, "we can wait to move the cattle for a few weeks."

"Not really, Chris," she said, giving in to a yawn that nearly cracked her jaw. "And you know it. If you tell me to take a nap, I think I'll tell you to go away."

"Okay then, I won't mention it."

"Great. Anything else you need to discuss?"

Chris pursed his lips. "Jack's been a whole lot of help the last few days. That man's not afraid of work."

The mention of his name made her sad. So sad. There was no other way to put it. The past few days, having him around, working, had been a dream.

One that she'd just ended.

Go back to your life. Let me have mine.

Who knew how long he might have stayed if she hadn't told him about her feelings?

Well, she scoffed, *long enough to sell the ranch. Let's not get too carried away here, Mia.*

"He'll be leaving soon," she said and grabbed a set of hand tools from the tack room.

"Mia." He sighed. "Just take a break—"

"I'll hit the sack early tonight," she promised Chris, whose blue eyes were worried.

"I can practically see through you, Mia."

Her fuzzy brain didn't have a quick comeback, so she scooted past him with a smile and mounted Blue, who shook back his mane and stomped with enthusiasm.

Five days without a ride and the boy was getting restless. Mia understood that.

"You sure you should be riding?"

"We'll be fine, Grandma," she said, frustrated with Chris's well-meaning concern. She was a big girl and his boss to boot. "Go back to your knitting."

Chris walked away, muttering under his breath. Mia knew she wasn't being all that smart, but the truth was, she needed a ride as much as Blue did. Her head was a mess and with any luck, a good, hard ride would clear it.

The high pasture would be silent and radiant with late-day sun. And best of all, she'd be alone.

JACK KNEW MIA was in the pasture without turning around. His gut, that world-class barometer, told him.

She's here.

He turned, looked over his shoulder to see her riding that old dun, Blue. She was gorgeous, sitting on top of her horse, her black ponytail lifted by the wind, fanning out across the brilliant blue sky behind her.

Her eyes were shadowed by the cap she wore, and that was fine. He didn't need to see her eyes to read her mood; it was all right there in the hard, high set of her shoulders.

The wagons had been circled, all her soft spots protected. The vulnerability that had so stunned him this morning was buried under the prickly outer shell she'd grown over the years. The shell he'd come to expect and… love?

Love, he thought, wishing he had some context. Some kind of organizational system, so he could look at each specimen and see if it was big enough or strong enough to keep him here. To keep her happy. Forever.

Because it didn't seem to be.

He didn't have those feelings, not for her, maybe not for anyone.

"I fixed your well," he said. She turned to look at it, then didn't turn back, as if it were simply easier than looking at him.

Don't be embarrassed, he wanted to say.

But it was too late, and she'd be more embarrassed if he said something.

"You shouldn't have any further trouble with it."

"Thank—" She cleared her throat and the tension between them filled the whole pasture, from endless sky to rocky ground. She emitted enough discomfort to rival the Sierras. "Thank you."

"I'm leaving tomorrow." The words were sticky in his throat and she finally turned to face him. Her lips, oh, those lips, parted in surprise.

Suddenly the reality of what he was doing sliced through him. He was losing Mia. His friend for his entire life. And that woman on the roof of the hotel in Santa Barbara, whom he'd only just met. Both of them would be gone.

Grief rippled over him.

Mia dismounted, but didn't come much closer. She wrapped her arms over her chest, as if keeping herself together.

"What you told me," he began. Good Christ, where was this emotion coming from? He felt his eyes burn. "About being in love with me—"

She turned, her cheeks red, her embarrassment a tangible pain and he didn't want that. Couldn't leave her ashamed of what she felt, not when he was the one who was embarrassed he couldn't return it. Not the way she deserved.

He leaped off the truck and crossed the

grass between them until he was right in front of her. Still, she didn't look at him. He watched her swallow, breathe, until he couldn't take it anymore and he touched her chin, her cheek, slid his fingers into her hair.

She gasped, her eyelids trembling, and he turned her head to face him, feeling things crack and split inside his chest.

"Thank you," he said into her brilliant eyes. He'd never forget those eyes. "For loving me. You're the only one who ever has."

Her face crumpled slightly as if bowing under the pressure of her feelings. He knew he should withdraw, take his hands away so she could get herself back together, but he didn't.

This was his last chance to touch her and he wasn't letting go until he had to.

"I'm going to take care of the tax problem," he said.

"What?" she asked, blinking up at him as if she didn't understand what she was saying. He knew his touch was distracting her; it was distracting him, too. Her cheeks, her skin, was the softest he'd ever felt. He ran his thumb over the skin near her lip.

Yep. The softest.

"It's the least I can do, Mia, and I know you want to argue with me about this because you're stubborn and proud, but you need this. So just take it."

Her eyes blazed

"I don't need it." She pulled away from him. "Once we sell the calves, the taxes are taken care of."

"Then use it to hire summer hands." Her eyes were full of emotion, the bedrock of her hardheadedness, the sharp edges of her resentment, the last white-hot embers of that love she'd felt for him.

"I'm not taking your money," she said.

"Please," he said, feeling as if his body were being turned inside out. "Let me do this for you. For all the years—"

"Fine," she snapped. "But only because I can't keep working my guys like this without facing mutiny. And I'm paying you back."

Fine. He'd take it any way he could get it.

"I'm also going to put some money aside for Dad, when he gets too sick for you to care for."

"That could be years—"

"Whenever it is, I just want you to have what you need to care for him."

Again, she nodded. "Thank you."

"I'm sorry, Mia," he said.

"You have nothing to be sorry for," she said. She didn't smile, had never been one for comfort, cold or otherwise. He remembered what she'd said in Santa Barbara—that he had always been a wuss when it came to the hard stuff. But she was the pro. Handling the hurt he'd unwittingly handed out, without ever letting on that she was in pain.

Regret burned through him again.

"I'm a big girl, Jack. I made my own decisions."

"If I had known..." He didn't finish the thought. Had no way of finishing it. If he'd known, would anything have been different? Truth be told, he probably wouldn't have married her.

"I would have died if you'd known," she said. "I didn't tell you for a reason. I've known, Jack, all along that you don't love me." She took a deep breath and then put a hand on the truck as she blew it out.

"Are you okay?" he asked, wishing he could console her.

"My husband is leaving me." She said it as a joke, even managed to smile, but he couldn't laugh. "Oh, come on, Jack, lighten up. It was always going to be temporary. My feelings don't change anything."

But what about mine? The thought erupted from nowhere, surprising the hell out of him. He stood there, staring into her face, wondering what was happening to him. He'd never worried about his feelings, because he so rarely had them.

But it was all changing. That jumble of emotion on the outskirts of his life was collapsing and the mess was epic.

"Thanks for fixing the well," Mia said, jerking her thumb over her shoulder.

Jack catalogued everything about her, as if she were a water table chart. He took her in, one piece at a time, so he could remember the whole of her better in the years to come—her wild hair, the bright eyes, the flushed skin. Her body, all those curves in such a compact space.

"Thanks for getting me out of that bedroom," he said. "For bringing me back to life."

"You would have done it on your own," she said. "In time."

"I don't know, Mia." He shook his head. "I was in a bad place."

"Then I'm glad I could help. I'm glad the ranch could help." She tried to sound bright, and it was close, but not convincing enough. She was trembling underneath her skin. "It was good you came here," she said. "Though you should talk to your dad before you go."

"What's the point?"

She gaped at him. Opened her mouth and then closed it again. Classic signs of a torn Mia, a Mia biting her tongue. "Just say whatever you want to say," he told her, reading her cues like a well-marked map.

"You…you need to deal with what your mother did to you," she said. "Your father, too."

He started, angry that she was making this about his childhood. His childhood was a distant memory. Forgotten. "What are you talking about?"

"You live in a cold world, Jack," she said quietly. "Maps and work and water tables. And I think your folks put you there. Science was safer than relationships. But if you ever want something lasting with someone—"

"I have you."

She swallowed and looked at her boots. "Not anymore," she whispered.

"I have…" He trailed off. Oliver. A numbing pain buzzed over his skin, separating him from his body.

He didn't have anyone. The minute he stepped off this ranch, he'd be alone. And for years, if he'd been asked, that would have been the way he wanted it.

Mia was right; science was safer than relationships.

"Where will you go?"

"I'm not sure," he said.

"Africa?"

"I think maybe you were right when you said I swoop in and change things without sticking around to see the results. The way we were drilling, going in every few months…I think that was doomed to failure for the same reason. Africa needs water, but they need organizations there for the long haul. And that's not me."

Her brows furrowed. "So what does that mean? For you?"

"I don't know, Mia."

She reached up, her cool fingers touching his cheek, and for a second he saw past the prickly exterior to the woman underneath. The woman in pain.

"You'll land on your feet, Jack. You always do."

Oh, it was too much. Too much. He kissed her. No warning; he didn't ask or apologize. He just did it. Pressed his lips to the soft chapped weight of hers, and when she moaned slightly, he pressed again, sliding his tongue past her teeth to lick at the sweetness of her mouth. She was stiff in his arms, but he pulled her closer until her hands dropped and he felt her curves against chest. His body woke up with a roar.

Mine, he thought, like some kind of barbarian. *My wife. My friend. Mine.*

Her hands touched his waist, fisting the fabric of his shirt as if holding on to a runaway horse.

She kissed him back, long and deep and hot and slow. Soul kisses like he'd never had. A thousand of them, over and over again. Until it wasn't enough. He needed more. This was goodbye, and he wanted all of her.

His hand slid down her back and around to her stomach, the taut muscles trembling under his hand. Taking a breath, waiting for her to push him away, he cupped the underside of her breast, but the sensation was muted beneath her jacket and shirt and bra.

So he tried again, finding the heat of her flesh beneath her clothes, pushing his hand up under her shirt and the elastic at the bottom of her sports bra until he held the sweet weight of her breast in his hand.

The nipple was hard under his fingers and he brushed his thumb over it, rolling it into his hand. She shook against him, her mouth opening on a low cry that tore away the last of his control.

The barbarian was loose and he lifted her up, sliding her onto the open bed of the truck, tipping her back so her open thighs cradled his hips. He could feel her heat through their denim and he rocked against her, desperate to hear her gasp, to feel her arch against him, to know that she wanted him as much as he wanted her. To know that when he left, she would grieve for him in all the ways he would grieve for her. He didn't stop, didn't let up until her body beat back against his.

Grinding herself against him, his entire body was electrified.

"Mia," he groaned against her lips, "My Mia, if this is goodbye—"

She went still. And it took him a second to catch on but he stopped, too, his erection pushing hard and tight against the crease of her jeans. One hand remained up the back of her shirt, curved over her shoulder, keeping her locked against him.

Please don't tell me to stop, he prayed, his mouth against her neck, waiting for her to speak.

"Let me go," she whispered. He could have cursed, but he did as she asked. Slipping his hands free, patting down her clothes, and then, feeling as if he were tearing off his skin, he stepped away. The cold air had no effect on the inferno raging through his body.

As soon as they weren't touching, Mia shot away from him, jumping off the back of the truck.

She stood so still, her back to him, and he couldn't bear it. "Mia," he breathed, putting his hand on her shoulder.

She jerked away. "Don't…just…give me a second."

A second? he thought, feeling mean and aroused and sad. *I'm leaving tomorrow. How many more seconds do you need?*

Her cap had been knocked off at some point and she took her time settling it back on her head. When she looked at him her eyes were deep wounds.

"I said goodbye to you once like that," she said. "I can't do it again."

The slump of her shoulders said more to him about how difficult this was than her words, and the last thing he ever wanted to do was cause her more pain.

"What if I stayed?" he blurted out and she gaped at him.

"What are you talking about?"

"I'm saying I…" God, what was he talking about? All he knew was that it hurt to leave her. He didn't *want* to leave her. "I'm saying, what if I stayed?"

"Here?"

"It's where you live. It's your home."

"You hate it here."

"It's growing on me."

"Please. You've just come out of your

room and you haven't said two words to your dad."

"I'm working on it, Mia," he said through gritted teeth. It wasn't the truth, but it wasn't totally a lie, either. "It's not easy for me."

"So, you stay and what? We…?"

"Try." He swallowed. "Being married."

Her eyes went wide, and he talked to fill the silence. "You love me, Mia. You said it yourself."

"The question is," she said, slowly and carefully as if every word were a sharp knife, an angry viper, "do you love me?"

"I…I feel something for you. I don't know if it's love. Frankly, I don't have much experience with that. But if I stayed, we could find out."

"Like an experiment?" she asked.

Oh, Lord, she got it. Amazing. "Yes!" he cried, reaching for her. "Exactly like that."

Something was coming over her face, something dark and stormy, and he realized that no, she didn't get it.

"Am I the experiment?"

"No, my feelings are," he said sheepishly.

"And what if your feelings don't hold up?"

she asked, crossing her arms over her chest. "What if we try and it doesn't work out?"

"Then I'll go, just like we're saying."

"No!" Mia cried and he realized he'd set off an avalanche of pain inside her, a whole wealth of emotion that he'd been clueless about. "I'm done being left by you, Jack. I'm done waiting for you to realize I'm part of your life. I have more pride than to let you…" She threw her hands up in the air. "Experiment! Are you kidding? Do you think so little of me?"

"No, God, Mia, no. I just…" Now he was getting angry. "I don't know how to do this."

"Be married or be divorced?"

"Either."

"Well," she snapped, "in your life, there's not much difference between the two."

"But what if there was a chance," he asked, "that this would work out?"

She shook her head, her lips white. "I don't care anymore." She was lying; he knew she was lying. "I'm tired of waiting for you, Jack. I won't do it anymore. You said you were leaving and I think…I think you should."

He couldn't push. He didn't have the right.

He'd blown every chance he'd ever had with her without knowing it.

"I'm…so sorry, Mia."

She nodded once and then held herself so still, as if she'd suddenly realized she'd been standing on glass and one move would send her falling to who knows where.

"Can you just go?" she whispered. "I need a minute."

Jack wanted to argue, but in the end he just nodded. "I'll leave you the truck—"

"I don't need the truck. I just need you to leave."

There was nothing else to say. Nothing else he could do. He climbed into the truck and drove away. Leaving her in the high pasture with her horse, twilight falling all around her.

CHAPTER TEN

BY DINNER, Jack was getting worried.

"She's a grown woman," Walter said, chasing peas around his plate as if they were greased pigs.

"Yeah, but it's been hours," Jack said, anxiety gnawing at his gut. He pushed away his plate, looking for allies in the other cowboys.

"I'm sure she's fine," Billy said. Tim nodded in agreement, not looking up from the last of the chicken pot pies.

Jack stared at Chris, who stared right back. "You go checking up on her," Chris said, "and she'll get pissed."

"But what if she's hurt?"

The cagey old cowboy nodded. "It's a quandary."

Screw quandaries, Jack thought. He couldn't eat until he knew Mia was safe. And if she was just riding Blue, or doing more work, or hell, crying her eyes out in the high pasture, she damn well knew better than to be gone for hours at a time.

"She doesn't have her cell phone?" Walter asked and Jack spun on the old man.

"She has a cell phone?"

Four grown men blinked up at him. "We all do," Chris said. "It's ranch regulation now."

I'm her husband and I don't know she has a cell phone?

"What's the number?" he demanded. Chris rattled off the number while Jack dialed on the home phone.

"This is Mia at Rocky M ranch, leave a message," her voice said.

After the long beep he said, "You need to call us. We're getting worried about you. It's 6:30—"

"Uh-oh," Tim said and Jack spun away from the wall-mounted phone, the message forgotten. The cowboys were up, staring out the big picture window at the barn in front. Even Walter was slowly getting to his feet.

"What?" Jack asked. His stomach was somewhere near his feet.

Chris turned, his face creased with concern. "Blue just walked into the yard," he said and then shook his head. "Without Mia."

"I knew it," Jack muttered, sweeping the keys to Mia's truck off the counter. If something had happened to her, it was his fault. He'd known she was too emotional, too tired to be riding down that ridge on her own.

And damn her for having every man in this house convinced she was invincible.

"Wait a second, boy," Walter said, grabbing his cane. "I'm coming with."

"I can go faster alone."

"You need another set of eyes," Walter said and for a second Jack saw a glimmer of his father in the old man's watery gaze. Implacable. Resolved. Right. "You watch the road. I'll watch the ravine."

Jack nodded and within moments he was back in Mia's truck, bouncing up the old fire road, his headlights cutting bright circles out of the dark.

Walter, on the other side of the bench seat, kept watch out his window, looking over the edge of the road for any sign of Mia. Once they got to the pasture, if they hadn't found her, Jack would walk back down, searching more carefully. The other men were taking a look at the barns and pastures.

Someone, at some point, would find her. And she'd probably be spitting angry and belligerent at all the fuss.

Please, God, he thought, his chest empty, *please let her be spitting angry and belligerent and not hurt. Not bleeding and broken at the bottom of a ravine.*

He'd just lost Oliver; he couldn't lose her, too.

"I have never in my life met anyone so stubborn," he muttered, and Walter shot him a sideways look.

"What?" Jack snapped.

"You're no slouch in the stubbornness department," Walter said, turning back to the window.

"I haven't risked my life—" He stopped. Because he had over and over again. God, was this how Mia felt every time he went to Africa? He rubbed a hand over his face.

"Her mother was stubborn," Walter said.

"Sandra?"

"Most stubborn woman I ever met."

"Worse than Mom?"

"Victoria was crazy," Walter said, shaking his head. "Big difference."

If it were any other time, Jack might have laughed. Instead, he focused on the road in front of them.

The darkness outside melted into the cab, broken only by the illuminated dials in the dashboard. It was getting colder out. Mia's jacket had been light. He remembered his hand under her thin shirt, against the warmth of her skin.

How long would she stay warm in the high country? If she was unconscious—

"There!" Walter yelled and Jack stopped the truck, peering into the darkness beyond his high beams. "Your side," Walter said, pointing out Jack's window. Jack saw the blur of a pale face as she turned and her left cheek caught the light. Slowly, she lifted a hand to shield her eyes from the glare of the headlights.

It was her.

He threw the truck in Park and hurtled into the night. She sat on a boulder, her legs splayed wide.

"Mia?" he said, dropping to his knees beside her. She blinked at him, her eyes unfocused. Not good. Unfocused eyes were never good. With shaking hands he turned her face so her right cheek caught the light from the truck.

It was red and black, sticky with blood.

Her cap was missing and he ran his fingers up under her hair, matted and thick with blood, until he felt a deep gash.

She winced and pulled away. "That hurts," she said, sounding like a child.

A need to protect her—to care for her—surged through him.

But it was all too late.

"What happened, Jack?" she asked, clearly confused. Lost.

He picked her up in his arms, feeling her chill through his denim jacket.

"I don't know," he said, easing her into the truck.

"She all right?" Walter asked as Jack slid her up against the old man.

Jack could only shrug.

"Hey, Walter," she said. "Victoria kick you out again?"

Walter and Jack shared a quick panicked look. And then Walter, showing more tenderness than Jack had ever seen, wrapped his arm around her and held her tight.

"Yep," Walter said. "You want to go for a ride?"

"Sure," she said, sounding sleepy.

"No sleeping!" Jack barked, putting the truck in gear and turning it around. He darted looks down at her face, watching her eyelids fight to stay open. "Come on, Mia. How about you tell me about the night of your high school graduation? Remember?"

"Of course I remember," she said. "It was my graduation."

"So, what happened?" he asked. The truck hurtled down the mountain and he tossed his cell phone toward his dad. "Call Chris," he told him. "Tell him we're going to the hospital."

"I was so happy you'd come home," she said, staring up at him. "Lucy said you wouldn't. That you probably wouldn't even remember what day it was, but I knew you'd come back for me."

Shit, he thought. Shit. Shit. Shit.

It was like looking at the past with different eyes and he hated it. He'd been the hero in his own story, getting out of that house, making it on his own. Never going back. In his memory he hadn't been so heartless.

She was quiet and he glanced sideways at her. "Hey now!" he said, shaking her leg. "Come on. What did we do that night?"

She opened her eyes and focused on him. For a second he saw some fear. Some clarity.

"I need you to stay awake," he told her, while Walter spoke quietly into the cell phone.

"My head hurts," she said. "And I'm freezing."

He cranked on the heater. "Graduation night, Mia—"

"You took me on the roofs," she said and he counted the miles to the nearest emergency room in Red Creek.

WALTER PUT ASIDE the cold brown water that passed for coffee in this hospital and watched his son pace the small waiting room from the TV in the corner to the magazine rack.

Six steps.

Turn.

Six steps.

Turn.

Honestly, the boy had to be getting dizzy.

"Sit down, Jack," he finally muttered. "You're making me seasick."

Jack collapsed into a plastic chair as if he'd been waiting for permission.

"You know this isn't your fault," Walter said, being sure to keep his eyes glued on the TV. It was that pretty dark-haired anchor lady on the Channel Three news.

"In what way is this not my fault?" Jack snapped. "I left her up there, Dad."

"She's a grown woman."

"Well, she sure as hell doesn't act like it."

"I suppose you'd be an authority on grown-up behavior?"

Jack opened his mouth and then shut it, as if realizing locking himself up in his room for five days was about as childish as it got.

"You know, Dad," he said, leaning forward, bracing his elbows on his knees. His eyes were narrow slits and Walter had a pretty good idea that whatever was coming wasn't going to be pretty. The boy was like a raccoon in a cage, all fired up with nowhere to go. "You're one to talk. How many times did you go to Al's Bar when Mom was on one of her rampages?"

"A lot," he answered, feeling a hot flush climbing up his skin. "I'm not proud of it."

"I suppose that makes it okay? Being sorry excuses your absence?"

"No," he said, turning away from the TV to face his son's damning eyes. "Nothing excuses the fact that I wasn't there for you when you needed me."

Jack blinked, a deer in headlights, trying to decide which way to jump.

"I kicked her out after that mess with Mia's family."

"I know."

"But you still didn't come home."

"Did you expect me to?" Jack asked. "Like getting rid of her, years too late would make me rush back here?"

Yeah. He had been stupid, hoping for that. "No," he said, "I suppose not."

The boy was silent for a long time and Walter watched him, drawing from a well of patience, deep and dark. Patience he'd never shown when Jack was a kid.

Jack stood, shaking his head, pacing a few feet.

"Mia says I need to deal with what Mom did to me," Jack said, staring up at the ceiling. All the pain he tried to hide covered him, as if he was a pack horse who'd never been given a break. "Can you believe that shit?"

Walter shifted in his seat, wishing he could be anywhere but here, but knowing his days of running from this were over.

"Your wife is a smart woman."

"My wife," Jack laughed. "My wife is kicking me off my own land."

"Thought that's what you wanted," Walter said. "To leave."

Jack pushed his hands through his hair, looking every inch a man who had no idea what he wanted.

Poor guy, Walter thought.

Walter figured there wasn't much to say, so he kept his mouth shut. Waiting for his son to get around to pushing those heavy weights off his back.

The silence deepened. Grew thick. It became hard to breathe and still he waited.

"Did you know she was hitting me?" Jack finally asked. "When I was a kid?"

It was the hardest thing Walter had ever done, owning up to his part in how traumatic

Jack's childhood must have been, but he nodded.

"I knew she raised her hand. But not how much. Or how bad."

"Why didn't you stop it?"

"At first it didn't seem so bad. You were a willful, stubborn boy—"

"Which of course makes it okay," Jack snapped.

"No. It doesn't. But she took on the discipline. I ran the ranch—"

"And drank. Don't forget the drinking."

Walter licked his lips. There was so much he wasn't proud of.

"I finally stepped in after that night you came home with me from town, with your clothes all torn. You'd been up on the roofs. Remember?"

Jack nodded, silent. His eyes wary.

"Anyway, I saw how she went after you…" Walter stopped. His hands were big, strong. His fingers wide, the middle three of both, bent sideways from the first knuckle from being broken long ago. He'd never hit his wife, never laid hands on her in that way, but it had been hard to control himself that night.

Jack'd been a big boy, but his fear, facing down Victoria, made him small. His own mother made him small. It wasn't natural.

Walter put a stop to it as quickly as he could, but Victoria had gotten a couple of good licks in with her belt. He'd sent Jack to Sandra to get cleaned up and he'd told Victoria that if she so much as touched their son in anger again, he'd send her away without a penny.

"She didn't hit you after that, did she?" Walter asked.

Jack thought for a minute. "No," he said, sounding surprised. "She didn't. Not like that."

Shame sizzled through Walter and he hated it. He hated himself. "I should have kicked her out years ago," he said. "But I didn't know what I'd do with you and I was so scared that she might get custody somehow. I mean, dads didn't get custody back then. Especially dads who spent most nights down at Al's."

"They did if their wives were nuts."

"But even that seemed to come and go," Walter said. He wasn't a smart man, never claimed to be, and the situation he'd gotten into with his wife made him feel even more stupid. "It was like a storm cloud would come over our house and she'd be this monster, and then it would leave and life would be normal again."

"For you!" Jack said with a dark laugh. "For me it was torture, waiting for the cloud to come back, wondering when it would." He shook his head. "It was hell. I almost got to the point that I liked the monster better. At least that was predictable."

"Dr. Meadows told me that he had medication that might make her better. Even her out. I got her to go see him, but she wouldn't take the pills."

This was the most they'd talked in years. Since Jack was a child and stopped clearing the fire road to the high pasture with him. That was one thing they'd always done together. Lighting and watching the fire— that had been their thing, once. Something Victoria couldn't touch, until she seemed to touch everything.

"She had to be bipolar," Jack said. "With borderline personality disorder and possibly paranoid schizophrenia."

Walter looked sideways at his son.

Jack shrugged. "I took a couple of psych classes in college."

"If I could change it—"

"You can't, Dad. It's the past. And it's over."

"I'm sorry, son—"

Jack held up his hand, anger climbing back onto his face. "Save it, Dad. Just...save it."

Walter nodded. The moment was over and he wasn't going to push. He'd gotten to say more than he thought he would.

The doctor, in a white coat and those green pajamas everyone seemed to wear in the hospital, came to stand in the doorway. "Jack McKibbon?" he asked.

Jack spun. "My wife?"

Walter did a double take at Jack's words, wondering if Jack even realized what he'd said or how he'd said it. Like *wife* was a word he used all the time.

"Your wife is fine," the doctor said, smiling to put them at ease in that way doctors did.

"Oh, thank God." Jack sighed.

"She's got a significant contusion on her brain and some pretty good bruising on her tailbone and shoulders and an ankle that isn't sprained, but she must have wrenched it fairly hard."

"She still doesn't remember what happened?" Walter asked. That seemed wrong. Dangerous. The fear he'd kept at bay all night, watching Jack wear a path in the linoleum, trickled down through his chest, bathing his heart in cold. "Is that bad? That's gotta be bad."

The doctor shook his head. "It's normal with head trauma. Don't worry, she'll probably remember in the next few days."

"She must have been thrown," Jack said, looking over to Walter who nodded. It made sense; everyone knew Blue was scared of snakes and that old fire road was thick with them in the spring.

"So, can we take her home?" Jack asked, and again Walter had to look at his son. Home? Had that word really come out of his mouth? Maybe Jack had some head trauma of his own.

"Yes," the doctor said, sounding doctorly all of a sudden. "But here's the thing. She needs to rest. And I mean rest, as in bed, feet up for a week. She needs to let her body heal."

"No problem," Jack said, and this time Walter did laugh.

"I'm sorry," Walter said, "but can you maybe give us some drugs or something that would make that easier? We've got rope, but I don't think that will help."

The doctor raised his eyebrows at Jack, who shook his head. "He's joking. We can manage without drugs or rope," Jack said. "She'll rest."

"Good," the doctor said. "You can sign discharge papers and pick her up on the second floor."

The doctor left and Jack grabbed his coat and stepped toward the door, ready to bring Mia back with orders for her to lie down for a week. As if that was going to work.

"Jack—"

"Dad, I know. I do. But we'll figure this out."

"We? Earlier today you were going to sell the ranch, now you're ready to be a nursemaid?"

"What do you want me to say? I can't leave."

"Yeah, and you and me can't keep that girl off her feet for a week."

Jack blinked, his brow crumpled. "You think we should leave her here?"

"No," Walter said, his palms sweating like a teenager's. And he knew that if anyone looked at him too long, they'd see right through him. Right to where his secret, his love and guilt, beat inside his chest. Victoria had been crazy, but she hadn't been totally wrong. She'd seen what he'd felt for another man's wife. "I'm saying we need reinforcements."

"Dad." Jack sighed. "I'm too tired for guessing games. If you have an idea, let's hear it."

"We need to call Sandra."

CHAPTER ELEVEN

MIA WOKE UP in her own bed, which was nice. The pain, however, was not. Her head felt like a bag of hammers and her body… oh, man, her body ached.

"Mia?" Jack's voice came gently out of the dark and she turned carefully to look at him. He sat in a chair by her bed, his stockinged feet up on the bottom corner of her mattress.

It was nice to see him. Comforting, even, and she knew it was all wrong. He was supposed to be leaving, because he didn't love her.

So, a smart woman wouldn't be so damn happy to see his socks at her bedside.

"You okay?" he asked, putting aside a small notebook computer. "Your head—"

"Hurts like hell," she muttered. "Along with the rest of my body."

"You remember what happened?"

She nodded. Blue had thrown her as soon as he'd heard the rattle from a snake underbrush. Or rather, Blue had leaped and Mia had been so wrapped up in her thoughts, she'd been caught with her pants down.

"I must have been out awhile," she said, trying to sit up. Lightning strikes of pain exploded through her body and she gasped.

Jack jumped out of the chair to help, carefully easing her across her sheets until her back was leaned against the pillows against her headboard.

But still he fussed, too close.

It was salt in her wounds. She would always be expendable to him. Her feelings were an experiment; no, not even that. *His* feelings were the experiment. She was…nothing.

"What are you doing?" she asked, wishing she could be just a little snappier. A little more forceful. But force had been concussed right out of her. Now she was just hurting. Head, heart and body.

"Helping," he said. "Can I get you something to drink?" He reached back over the edge of the bed. "I have water." He lifted up a glass. "Or tea." He lifted up a thermos. "Two sugars, loads of milk."

That was the way she liked her tea.

She blinked at him, surprised he knew.

Oh, no, she told herself, *it's just tea. And you've been drinking it around him for years. Don't get too excited.*

"Tea," she said, because her throat was dry and her brain felt like wadded-up tissue.

He unscrewed the stainless-steel lid and poured the caramel-colored liquid into it. Steam wreathed his face and the smell made her stomach growl.

"You're hungry?" he asked with a smile.

And it was too much, him sitting there as if they hadn't argued. As if she hadn't told him to leave.

"When are you going?" she asked, and his hand paused as he passed her the cup. She took it from him, careful not to touch him. She didn't even look at him.

"I can't leave you now," he said.

Her fingers flinched and tea spilled over the quilt. She used the wrist of her long-sleeved T-shirt to clean it up.

"You need to rest," Jack said. "Really rest. Like in bed."

"And you're sticking around to make sure I do it?"

"Someone has to," he said.

"I don't need a nurse," she said. "Or a keeper. Or—" she looked right at him "—a husband. Not anymore."

Jack's face was dark and she knew she'd hurt him. Part of her was glad. A little reciprocated pain for all she'd felt over the years.

"Well, you need another guy out in the fields, if you're moving the cattle to the north pasture."

Mia bit her tongue, wishing it wasn't true.

"Sure," she finally said, sounding ungrateful even to her own ears. "I could use another hand."

He gave her a long look, demanding she try again. But nicely this time. She stuck out her tongue.

"We've called your mother," he said, laughing a little.

"What?" she cried, jerking upright, and the pain ricocheted from her toes to the ends of her hair.

She groaned and Jack went back to fluffing her pillows.

"She and Lucy will be here in two days."

"No," she moaned. "Tell me you're kidding."

Jack looked confused, the poor idiot, so unaware of the shit storm he just unleashed on his own head. "The ranch could use her," Jack said. "I really don't understand what the problem is."

"The problem is, Jack, my mother—my very Catholic mother—doesn't understand why our marriage isn't real. Why we're not giving her grandchildren as we speak."

She put a hand to her forehead. Her head felt as if it were going to burst under the pressure.

"And Lucy." She sighed. She loved her family. Adored them. Missed them terribly since they'd left. But she didn't need them to come here to take care of her. Not while Jack was here. It was all difficult and confusing enough without adding her mother's hope and her sister's cynicism to the mix. "Lucy wants to kill you, Jack. She's said so herself. In fact, I bet they're not even coming up here for me. They're coming up here to get their hands on you."

Jack rubbed his neck, looking all too handsome and close and concerned. "It'll be fine," he said.

She managed to laugh. This could be fun, actually, watching her sister and Mom putting the gears to Jack. "I hope so," she said, taking a sip of tea. "For your sake."

THE NEXT NIGHT, Mia crept out of bed, holding herself very still, so that no part of her body screamed out in pain and brought Jack running like Florence Nightingale.

It had been one day since being tossed off Blue, and she was going out of her mind. There was only so much television a woman could watch. Only so many books she could start and then get bored with.

And she knew that all the calving data in her notebooks needed to be transferred into the computer. That was something she could do; she could even put her feet up while she did it.

The clock on her bedside table read 10:30, and the house was quiet. Maybe no one would even know if she left her room for more than a bathroom break.

She turned the knob on her door and something jangled and thumped against the other side of the door. She jerked the door open to find her old bridle, the one done up in Christmas bells, looped around the doorknob.

Bastard!

The bedroom door next to hers opened and Jack, wearing nothing but an old pair of sweats, stepped out into the hallway.

He grinned, scratching his belly. "Going somewhere?" he asked.

"This is a little much, isn't it, Jack? Why don't you just lock me in?"

"No locks," he said with a shrug, as though the idea had occurred to him and it was simply unfortunate he couldn't go with his first choice.

The door across the hall opened and Walter appeared in the dark, wearing a pair of faded blue pajamas.

"It worked," he said with a sly grin that Mia truly did not appreciate.

"Told you it would," Jack said.

Walter nodded and turned himself around without the help of a cane or his walker. She was surprised to see how much improvement he'd made in the past two weeks. He was practically a different man, and she'd been so busy she barely noticed.

"Go to sleep, Mia," Walter said over his shoulder and shut the door behind him.

"You heard the man," Jack said, covering a yawn with his fist. She wished Jack would cover up his chest with a damn shirt. Honestly, what was a hydro-engineer doing with six-pack abs?

He was crowding her in the doorway, forcing her to step back into her room, but she wasn't about to be herded.

"Come on, Jack," she protested. "I'm so bored."

"Watch TV," he said.

"Have you watched TV lately?" she asked. "Nothing but bad talent shows and half-naked people in hot tubs kissing each other."

He waggled his eyebrows. "That sounds all right to me."

He put his hand on her arm, gripping her elbow to help her turn, and the contact made her body ring out like the Christmas bells on that bridle.

See, she thought, *see what too much television will do to a woman? Give her body ideas it has no business having.*

She pulled away to give her unruly body a chance to simmer down. "You know I can sit at the computer just as well as I can sit in this room."

"Computer?" he asked, pulling the blankets down off her bed, revealing the white sheets.

"The calving data needs to be entered into the system and I—"

Jack shook his head, making the wild rooster tail of his hair wave. His hair had gotten long since Santa Barbara, longer than she'd ever seen it. It made him look disreputable. She clenched her hands into fists against the urge to push them into that thick blond mess, feel the silky strands against her skin.

"You want to work?" he asked. "You know that's against the rules."

"It's computer work! It's not like I'm herding cattle."

"Back in bed, Mia," he said, shaking the blankets as if she were a bull. They stared at each other a long time, but she wasn't about to go willingly back into her jail, not without some kind of concession.

"Okay." He sighed, finally. "I'll put the program on my laptop and you can enter the data in here tomorrow."

Not bad as far as compromises went.

"All right," she said, "but I'm bored now." She sounded whiny, even to her own ears, but she was desperate.

"It's ten-thirty," he said. "Sleep."

"I slept all day."

Jack took a deep breath and again she tried not to look at his body. It was impossible. He was gorgeous, sleek and smooth, his chest was defined and strong, his arms thick with surprising muscles.

And his sweatpants hung on an ass she wanted to take a bite out of.

"You know, I've changed my mind," she said, slightly scared of this renewed attraction, the intimacy of her bedroom and the thick night around them. No good would come of this. "Forget it."

Her aching tailbone was beginning to think those white sheets and soft bed looked pretty good, so she crawled in carefully and yanked the blankets out of his hand.

He stared down at her, and Mia felt his gaze, like it was his hand, sweeping across her forehead and over her hair. He wanted to touch her, his intent was such a force, she could barely stand it.

And for a second, the stupid parts of her brain and the starved parts of her body joined forces and she thought, what the hell? He was here, they were married, she was bored out of her skull and it wasn't as if they could do all that much considering the pain she was in—what harm could come of it?

Well, plenty. But the scales were beginning to tip out of balance and the harm didn't seem so bad in the face of how much she wanted to touch him and be touched.

Loved, somehow.

Jack stepped away, his eyes on hers, and she wondered in a weird spellbound state if he was going to shut the door and climb into this bed with her. If that was how the boredom of this night would be dealt with.

Once again, stupid and starved got a little happy and her body started to hum.

But then he was out the door, brushing past the bells and making them ring.

For the best, she told herself, adding the small hurt to the piles of pain and unhappiness her relationship with Jack had brought her.

And just as quickly, he was back in her doorway, carrying a small case.

"You still play chess?" he asked, his eyes bright, his smile the sweetest she'd ever seen. He looked so much like the boy she'd fallen in love with that it stung.

Why did this feel more dangerous than touching him? They'd played a hundred games of chess, thousands. The smart part of her brain that had been somehow silent when she'd wanted to rub herself all over him decided to chime in.

Don't do it.

Jack took her silence as a yes and stepped into the room, pulling the chair up closer to her bed. He opened the travel chess set to reveal the small black and white pieces nestled in little compartments.

Jack went still, looking down at the game as if it wasn't what he expected. As if a snake lay curled up on the magnetic board.

"Jack?" she asked.

"Oliver—" His voice cracked and he cleared it. "Oliver and I played." His thumb brushed over the white queen. "At night."

Jack's grief was a presence in the room and she could sense him withdrawing, watched him start to fold up the set so he could go back to his room and do whatever he'd been doing the week he first came to the ranch.

Grieving. Hiding.

And that wasn't good for anyone. As dangerous as it might be to her heart for them to play chess the way they had when they were kids, it was far more dangerous for Jack to go back to hiding.

She put her hand on the board. "I'm black," she said, pulling the pieces from their compartment. She set them up, pretending not to watch him, but so aware of him she could feel his emotions in the air. His grief and sorrow, his indecision. Everything.

And she could tell, by the way he sat, by the way he watched her and finally by the way he started to set up the white pieces, that his grief had turned to gratitude.

"Let's see if you've gotten any better," she said. "Somehow I doubt it."

He laughed and the trash talk began.

JACK HADN'T BEEN SO HAPPY in…months. He felt a certain ease that he didn't entirely recognize. A looseness in his muscles that indicated a state of relaxation that was foreign to him.

Santa Barbara was the last time he'd felt like this. And before that... God, he couldn't remember. Happiness wasn't anything he sought. There'd been no place for it in his life. There had been his work and the sub-categories of that: Africa. Oliver. The drill.

It had seemed like so much, a mountain he had to climb every day, an ocean of paper-work and problems that only he, Jack McKibbon and no one else, could solve.

It had allowed him, he supposed, to hide. To run away from even trying to find happiness. To protect him from the disappointment of never actually getting it.

And looking down at the crown of Mia's head, he knew, in a way he'd been hiding from her.

A tension awoke in his belly, an aware-ness of her body, the loose T-shirt that pulled across her breasts, revealing the rigid peak of her nipple. Her arms, tanned and strong, looked so sweet and tender poking out of the too-big sleeves.

His wife.

The celibacy he'd lived with and grown accustomed to wasn't fitting so well right now. All he could do was sit here and think of Santa Barbara and the way her breasts had felt in his hands. The way her tongue had tasted in his mouth. How tight and hot and sweet she'd been.

He coughed and rearranged himself in his chair, crossing his legs.

You're an ass, he told himself. *The woman has a concussion and you're sitting here with a boner! Get a grip.*

"I'm hurrying, I'm hurrying," she grumbled, moving her rook sideways.

He was barely paying attention to the game and he knew she'd win. She usually did. He liked chess, but Mia had a brain for it like he'd never seen. Oliver had been good, liked to brag about winning some junior championships in England. But he'd been a hack compared to Mia.

Thoughts of Oliver brought the grief and guilt back like a black curtain, shutting out his contentment.

"Hey, Jack," Mia said, breaking him from his thoughts. Thank God. He moved his king two spots to his right, but it was such a weak move that Mia put the piece back.

"Castling? That was bad," she said. "Even for you. Try again."

He concentrated, finally seeing her bishop for the threat it was, and moved his knight to counter.

"Can I ask you a question?"

"Shoot," he said.

"Were you really…"

He glanced up at her, noticing the fire-engine–red blush on her neck and face and sat back, crossing his arms over his chest. This ought to be good.

"Was I really, what?"

"Celibate," she blurted. "All these years?"

He took a deep breath. "Like a monk."

"But you never tried…anything with me. I mean, you said on that roof that you'd been thinking of me like that, so I know it wasn't just the dress or the wine."

"It wasn't the dress or the wine," he agreed softly, the game totally forgotten. "I'd been thinking about you like that since you were fifteen."

Her eyes widened and her mouth fell open.

"I felt like a pervert, not just because you were so young, but because you were my friend. So I told myself that I would never do anything, not unless you started it."

"Fifteen?" she asked and he nodded. "Wow."

The years they'd wasted were enough to make a guy sick. Amazing. He was a scientist who'd somehow failed to observe his own wife.

"Can I ask you a question?" he said.

She nodded, looking so uncomfortable he was torn between hugging her and pressing her back against the mattress and showing her all the many ways he'd thought about her over the years.

"You weren't a virgin that night—"

"Did you expect me to be?"

"No! No, I didn't. But I never heard about any boyfriends or whatever—"

"Was I supposed to call you and tell you I got laid?"

He shook his head. This was stupid. "Never mind, it's none of my business."

"You're right, it's not." She was so small curled up against a pile of white pillows. The bruising on the side of her face made her look impossibly tough and fragile at the same time. But that was Mia for him.

And being her husband gave him no right to her sexual history. Her secrets were her own. He looked back down at the chessboard and the mess of black and white pieces.

"Whose turn is it?"

"Bill Winters," she said and he looked up, slack-jawed. "We got together the night after my high school graduation. I told myself when you left that night that you clearly didn't feel anything and it was time to get on with my life."

"By having sex with Bill Winters?" Strange that he was jealous over something that had happened twelve years ago.

"We dated for a while afterward. He was a nice guy and he liked me."

"I was a nice guy and I liked you!"

Her eyes flashed in anger. "You didn't let me in on that little secret, Jack. You kept it to yourself."

He took a deep breath. "I know. I'm sorry. It's just…strange, I guess, to think of you with someone else."

"You weren't a virgin in Santa Barbara, either, Jack."

"I felt like one," he said. He picked up one of her captured pawns, rolling it between his fingers instead of reaching for her.

"Five years of celibacy will do that to a

guy, I suppose," she said, trying to make a joke of something that wasn't funny.

"You did it to me, Mia. You. You made me feel…different. The sex felt different. Hell, the whole night felt different."

She nodded, her head bent, and he stared at the curve of her cheek, telling himself that what he wanted to do was a mistake. In fact, the way he felt right now, the combustibility in the air, the only thing that wouldn't be a mistake would be leaving.

But he wasn't about to leave.

"I'm sorry we wasted so much time," he whispered.

"Me, too, Jack," she breathed.

He pushed the chess set out of the way and leaned down to her. He knew she was hurting and he wasn't going to force his way into her bed, but he wasn't leaving without touching her.

He needed this—the physical proof of their connection—and he was pretty damn sure she did, too.

His fingers touched her cheek, a small spark popping between them, and she smiled, awkwardly.

"Let me kiss you," he said.

"Jack—"

"Just a kiss, Mia."

She didn't say anything, her whiskey eyes staring up at him, watching him as he inched forward and pressed his lips to hers. Her eyelids shut on a soft sigh and he melted into her, absorbed by the sweetness and spice of Mia.

He didn't want to push, was unsure of how far her welcome extended, but when she opened her mouth against his, the tip of her tongue licking at his lips, he wanted to growl in triumph.

Instead, he let her in, let Mia all the way in. He opened himself up and hoped that she would find a home somewhere inside the mess of his life and heart.

Because he needed her. He always had, he'd just been too stupid to know it.

He pulled away from the sweet kiss, even though it was counterintuitive to everything he wanted to be doing.

"You're hurt," he said and after a moment she nodded. "Can you sleep?" he asked, and she laughed a little.

"Eventually." She looked up at him. Her eyes radiant, her face so lovely it actually hurt. "Thanks," she said. "For the game. It's been a long time."

"We'll play again," he said. "Tomorrow."

She shook her head. "Tomorrow night my mom and Lucy will be here."

"And we can't play chess?"

She stared at him for a long time. "My mom and sister both know this marriage isn't real, but it hasn't stopped my mother from hoping—"

"I told you I would stay," he said in a rush. "We could try to make this real."

She shook her head, her eyes dry as a bone. "I've got no more hope to be lifted, Jack," she said. "I can't manage to care anymore. I've been left by you too many times to count."

"I didn't know," he said in his defense.

"Would it have been so different if you had?" she asked.

He couldn't lie to her. "I don't know."

"I do," she said quietly. "I've always known everything was second to your work, your… dream. And just because you no longer have that dream doesn't mean I'm ready to believe I can take its place. I think you're searching, Jack, and I'm in the right place at the right time."

"It's not like that."

"It feels like it is, Jack. And that's enough for me. When my family gets here, I'm going to tell them we're getting a divorce and then…maybe we should just keep our distance."

Keep our distance.

Funny how he'd managed to do that for years without even trying, and now it seemed impossible.

CHAPTER TWELVE

JACK BOOTED UP his laptop for her and showed her the icon for her calving worksheet. He was so close Mia could smell the sunshine and pine on his skin; the heat of his body bathed the side of her face, her right hand.

"You got it?" he asked, not exactly cold, but not the Jack who'd played chess with her last night.

Don't you dare feel bad, she told herself. *Don't you dare. That man hurt you more times than you can count and the second you decide to protect yourself for once, you feel bad?*

Don't be such a girl, Mia.

"I think I can manage."

"You have your notebooks?" he asked, stepping away from the bed. He wore his old cowboy hat, the brown one with the black band. He said he'd found it in the barn this morning, surprised that it was still kicking around.

She'd just nodded, as if she hadn't hidden it there almost the minute he'd left for college. Worn it when missing him had been so powerful she couldn't stand herself.

Wearing the hat changed Jack McKibbon, mutated his mild-mannered scientist persona into something more primal and earthy. He looked sharp and focused.

Painfully hot.

"Chris is bringing them to me," she said.

"Call my cell if you need anything," he said. "I'm heading over to the Stones'."

"Everything okay?" she asked.

"Jeremiah had a question about the alfalfa irrigation system. Told him I'd take a look at it."

"Look at you," she said with a smile, and then hated herself for smiling. "You just can't resist a water problem."

"Well." Jack's smile sliced through the shadows under his hat. "Jeremiah's less likely to bomb me, so I figured I'd do what I can."

He walked out, leaving behind currents and eddies that teased and tugged at her, pulling and pushing her off balance. And she could only sit there, aching and battered, and wish he'd never come back to this ranch.

Chris knocked on her door a few minutes later.

"Come on in," she said and the old cowboy took a tiny step into the room, looking highly uncomfortable to be there.

She grinned at her friend. "You're kidding, right?"

"Christ, Mia," he said, unable to look at her. "You're in your pajamas."

"Which happens to be an old flannel shirt. It's not like I'm here naked."

"Still," he said, taking another step into the room. "It's not right. Here." He handed her the three notebooks she'd filled with calving information and notes.

"Thanks." She took the notebooks and Chris hightailed it to the door. "Wait."

He groaned, but turned to face her. "How is Jack working out?" she asked.

Chris frowned. "Jack? Fine. He's got the boys clearing the fire road so we can move the herd."

That was surprising. "He's not trying to boss you, is he?"

Chris's smile was brief. "Well, he is the boss and frankly, so far, I agree with everything he's wanted to do." He shrugged. "It's his ranch."

"Yeah, which he hates."

Chris sighed. "Can I please go?"

"Yeah, yeah," she said, waving him out of the room. "Be free."

Chris left and now it was just her and Jack's laptop. She searched for the shortcut icon on the desktop and got sidetracked by a document entitled I Take Full Responsibility.

Without a second thought, or really without giving herself a chance to have a second thought, she clicked on the document.

I take full responsibility for the mistakes that were made by the team on our return trip to El Fasher. The death of Oliver Jenkins and the destruction of the pump and drill might have been prevented had I informed the team of the errors on the new set of maps. I knew the permanent compound was being built too far from the new pump site and that should there be an attack, we wouldn't be able to get to safety in time.

I was aware of the problems the night of the university cocktail party in Santa Barbara and didn't notify anyone due to my absorption in my personal problems. With my heartfelt apology I tender my resignation to the university.

Mia stared dumbfounded at the screen on her lap. Was he insane? she wondered. Jack was going to take responsibility for a militia *bombing?*

Did he have a God complex, or what?

She remembered that night a few weeks ago when she'd fallen asleep in the chair in the living room. He'd said, yelled really, it was all his fault and she'd forgotten about it.

But he'd been serious. He blamed himself for Oliver's death.

"Oh, Jack." She leaned back against the pillows. Picking him out of her life, like splinters out of her skin, would be so much easier if she didn't care so damn much.

That he carried around this unjustified load swamped her with sympathy, with unwanted affection, because it was so totally like him to take on that responsibility. The too-big responsibility, the unreasonable and unnecessary responsibility, was Jack's specialty.

Marrying his best friend so she could stay on the ranch she loved. Bringing water to a nation dying of thirst. Taking responsibility for a senseless, mindless act of terrorism, because he felt like the blame needed to be put somewhere.

His mother had done that, put the weight of the world on his shoulders.

And you are not the woman to make it right, she told herself. *You are not the wife he wants, not really.*

Taking her own advice to heart, she closed the file and opened up her program and began inputting the calving data. But she couldn't focus. Jack had written that he'd known the about the map problem that night in Santa Barbara and claimed to have forgotten about it because of "personal issues"... Was *she* the personal issue?

He'd called and emailed relentlessly for weeks after they'd made love. And she'd dodged every call.

Oh, her stomach twisted between curiosity and sick, terrible dread.

MIA WAS IN HIS ROOM. In his bed, actually. Which would be wonderful if he and Mia were a normal married couple. But they weren't. They were keeping their distance and now she was in his bed, making the sheets smell like her.

Jack had enough problems sleeping without being haunted by Mia-scented sheets.

"You're supposed to be resting," he said, tossing his hat onto his desk. It skidded across the bare surface and fell into her lap.

"I am," she said, tucking the hat on her head, tipping it over one eye. "Note my reclining position."

Oh, he'd noted it. She looked like some kind of lewd cowboy fantasy in that hat.

He'd had a busy day. Stone's alfalfa field irrigation system was pretty much shot. And when Jack had stopped by to help the guys clear the fire road, his father had been there in the middle of things, like the man he'd been. He'd been leaning against the truck, his hat down low over his eyes and for a second Jack'd had a good memory of this place. A decent one, of the two of them clearing that road when he was a kid.

And he stood there on that road with the past he'd thought was dead coming back to life around him. But different somehow. Changed.

Mia wasn't the girl he knew her to be.

He couldn't cast his father as the villain. Not entirely.

And Jack felt himself changing along with his memories.

So now he smelled like smoke and fire, and he was confused.

And having Mia here wasn't helping. Trying not to look at her only seemed to make him more aware of her; her black curls were stark and erotic against the snowy-white pillow case. The flannel shirt she slept in wasn't buttoned all the way up and he saw far too much of her throat, the elegant rail of her collarbone, the mysterious valley between her breasts.

She wore a pair of boxer shorts, and her long caramel-colored legs were stretched out over his unmade bed, her thin ankles crossed. Her toes naked and practically taunting him.

He wanted to eat her, lick her. Spread himself on top of her like butter and melt right into her skin.

"Why aren't you in that reclining position in *your* room?" he snapped, yanking his filthy T-shirt over his head and firing it into the corner with the rest of his filthy T-shirts.

"Because I want to talk to you," she said. He noticed, because he noticed everything about her, that she went a little wide-eyed at the sight of his chest.

Good.

He undid the top button on his jeans, ready to make her eyes pop right out of her head.

"What are you doing?" she squeaked.

"I need to take a shower," he said as the other button slid free.

"Can you keep your clothes on while I talk to you?"

"I suppose it depends on what you're saying." He grinned at her blush. Damn it, but his mood was improving. Mia Alatore blushing was about the strangest thing he'd ever seen, like seeing a dog in pants, but it was pretty, too.

"I want to talk to you about the bombing."

He unfastened the rest of the buttons all at once. "Sorry," he said, pushing the pants down his legs, "not interested."

"Stop!" she cried, all but shielding her eyes. "Stop, please, Jack, I just want to talk."

She was taking quick glances at him in his underwear and then looking away for a second, before her eyes would come wandering back.

"Well, I don't," he said. "Not about Africa."

He tucked his thumbs in the waistband of his boxers as if he was about to pull them down and Mia's eyes lurched up to his.

"I read your statement to the university," she blurted.

That gave him pause. "Snooping around?"

She nodded, not even embarrassed.

"How can you believe that the bombing was your fault?" she asked.

"I don't believe the bombing is my fault," he said. "I believe the fact that Oliver is dead and Devon and I were hurt is my fault."

"You didn't make the decision to build the compound so far from the pump site."

"No, but I sure as hell didn't correct it, though, did I?"

"And neither did anyone else, Jack. And would it have mattered if you did?" she asked. "The place was bombed down to nothing. Was the compound even left standing?"

He nodded, feeling bile rise in his throat, wishing he'd kept his clothes on. "The storage area was ruined, but the living quarters were practically untouched. If we'd been able to get inside when we heard the planes coming, Oliver would be alive."

"Oh, Jack." She sighed, and he knew she understood. His guilt wasn't for nothing. There were ramifications for mistakes that he'd made.

And sure, Oliver and Devon might have noticed the problem with the build site and chimed in, but no one else had until it was too late. And by then they'd just decided to do the best they could.

"But what if you weren't able to get inside?" she asked.

He stared at her. "I'm not following."

"You can't second-guess everything. It's a war over there, Jack. You could have told someone about the problems with the map, but maybe that would have created another problem. Perhaps, if the compound had been placed correctly, it would have been leveled. Maybe you'd be dead instead of Oliver. Maybe all of you would be dead."

Jack turned around, tired of this conversation. His towel hung over the doorknob to his closet and he grabbed it, throwing it over his shoulder. "I'm done talking about this," he said and left her in his bed to go take a shower.

He'd just stepped under the hot spray when the curtain was jerked aside.

"Jesus, Mia," he snapped, yanking part of it back to cover his crotch. "What the hell are you doing?"

"Trying to talk some sense into that thick head of yours. This is not your fault. You don't need to take responsibility for every bad thing that happens."

"Go lie down—"

"No!" she snapped. Mist sprayed her face and hair. The front of her shirt got damp, outlining the full slope of her breasts, the soft point of her nipple

His anger toward her turned into something else, something dark and desperate.

"Your mom did this to you," she said. "How many years as a kid did you do everything you could to make her happy? You made her your responsibility."

He ignored her and that made her even more angry.

"It's not your fault that you're alive and Oliver's dead," she said, her eyes bright and hot, and the fever in his belly grew. Behind the shower curtain, his erection throbbed.

"Do you hear me, Jack?" she asked.

No, he thought, staring as the white parts in that flannel shirt grew translucent.

"Get out of here, Mia, before I show you how alive I really am," he said. She gaped as if she didn't understand and so he dropped the shower curtain, standing there on fire for her.

Her lips fell open on a small gasp, and in front of his eyes, her nipples hardened, pressing against the wet flannel.

She stared up at him and he stared back, unapologetic.

You're my wife, he thought. Not long ago, the word had meant nothing. But now he wanted to bury his hurt and confusion and guilt in her soft body. He wanted her to take his pain away. To comfort him, the way husbands and wives were supposed to.

He could see she was torn. Her love for him was probably more hurtful than it had ever been, and he was a selfish bastard to torture her. But he was feeling pretty damn tortured himself.

"Run away," he said, grabbing the soap from the ceramic shelf it sat in. He lathered his hands and ran them over his chest, down his stomach to his erection. He stroked himself, gritting his teeth against the pleasure and agony. "Go," he taunted her. "Back to your room. Where you don't ever have to worry about losing anything because you never go after what you want."

"What would you know about it, Jack?" she spat.

"I know you married me and never told me you loved me. I know that I'm here now, and you're still too scared to try. I think it's easier to love me when I'm far away," he said. "It's easier for you to live on this ranch, to bury yourself in work, to nurse all the hurts over all the years, instead of taking a risk and trying for something real."

She gaped at him and he turned to face the

water, rinsing off the soap. "Honestly, Mia, go away."

He snapped the shower curtain shut in her face.

HER MOTHER AND SISTER arrived late the following night having left Los Angeles after Sandra's church meeting. Walter tried to wait up with her, but he finally gave in around one, leaving her alone stretched out on the living room couch. Jack had come in after dinner, eaten Gloria's pot roast over the sink in the kitchen and then gone to bed.

Mia would have felt invisible but for one long glance that about melted the clothes right off her body. The most sexual, erotic thing she'd ever experienced had been making love with Jack on that Santa Barbara rooftop.

Until last night.

Watching him touch himself destroyed her. Ruined her. Tore down every single wall she had built around her feelings and now things were running amok. Some dark well of fantasy, of sexual deprivation, had opened up inside her head and she was consumed by thoughts of Jack. And her.

And naked, filthy sex acts. Things she'd

heard about but never fully understood or didn't believe were physically possible. She wanted it all. And she wanted it with Jack.

He'd walked down the hallway to his room tonight and it was all she could do not to follow. Her family be damned, she was a woman. And suddenly she had needs.

But those needs were a complication. The lust and the fantasies and the constant tingle in her sad, neglected lady parts were only making an already tenuous situation impossible.

Mia needed to be back on her feet, back out in the barn so Jack could leave.

His words from last night, the way he'd taken her life and rearranged it, made every support beam that held up her world seem fragile and silly. Insubstantial.

She needed her sister here with her long memory and clearheaded cynicism to remind her that Jack McKibbon and her feelings for him were toxic. Poisonous.

Delicious, delicious poison.

She dozed off after Walter left and woke up to the sweet smell of her mother—roses and cumin. Home.

Mia lingered in that place between sleep

and being awake, where her body was thick and fuzzy and the past and present were separated by cobwebs.

"Sweet girl," her mom said, and Mia knew everything was going to be okay. The mess of her life would be put to order.

"Where's that husband of yours?" Lucy's acidic voice asked.

Or not.

CHAPTER THIRTEEN

IT TOOK A WHILE for Jack to realize that Jeremiah's eyes had glazed over.

"Sorry," Jack murmured, replacing a pipe with the section he'd taken apart. "I get a little carried away."

"Who doesn't?" Jeremiah asked with a laugh. "I mean, double cross filtration systems are fascinating stuff. My question is, can you fix my irrigation rig?"

Jack shook his head. It wasn't that he couldn't; it was that he wouldn't be around to do it. Fixing the irrigation system would take more time than he had left on the ranch. He was going back to the university in two weeks. By then Mia would be on her feet and his marriage would be over.

"Yeah," Jeremiah said, "probably below your pay grade." Jack didn't correct him; he didn't have the inclination to explain the mess of his life.

"Well." Jeremiah sighed and stretched, his lean body curling and uncurling. "Guess I'll have to find someone else."

Jack didn't tell him, but the former rodeo star had a Cheerio in the hair over his ear.

"Do you miss your old life?" Jack asked, loath to go home despite the setting sun. Sandra and Lucy had arrived late last night, and Mia's warnings about the women looking for his blood were beginning to make him nervous. "The rodeo?"

Jeremiah pushed his hand through his hair and ran into that crusty Cheerio. "Like you wouldn't believe," he said with a smile, flinging the Cheerio into the grass. "You? You miss saving the world?"

"No," Jack answered right away. "Not at all. But…I miss the science. Using my brain to solve problems."

"Herding cows doesn't compare?"

Jack smiled. "That's good, too," he said. "Surprisingly good. I like the guys and the work is honest and hard, which is more than I would get most days from the university. Being head of research involved pushing a lot of paper around a desk."

"And getting bombed."

"That, too." He looked down at his boots, the dirt that covered them. "It's no wonder I'm ready to be done with it."

"Hey, I think it's great you're back," Jeremiah said. "I mean, with your dad being sick and, you know, your wife being hot… it's good you're home."

Home. Is that where he was? Because it felt like limbo. Purgatory.

Purgatory because his hot wife wanted nothing to do with him.

He thought about what she'd said the other night, about taking the place of his dream. She couldn't have been more wrong. Mia and his work occupied two different sections of his life. Two different places. Wanting one had nothing to do with the other.

"I better go," Jeremiah said. "I need to pick Eli and Casey up at day care."

Jack shook his head, laughing.

Jeremiah's smile faltered at the corners. His blue eyes were dark and Jack realized all was not well with his old friend.

"Sometimes I wake up," Jeremiah said, "and I don't even know who I am anymore."

Oddly enough, Jack felt just the opposite.

He woke up and knew exactly who he was; he just didn't know where he fit.

THE HOUSE HAD BEEN QUIET when Jack left at dawn and when he returned the scene was very different. He took off his boots in the mudroom and stepped into a party.

Keith Urban was playing; Lucy, the gypsy, was singing along, mesmerizing Tim and Billy who sat slack-jawed at the table. Walter and Mia were doing something with a bowl of limes and the air smelled…amazing.

"Jack!" Sandra, a small, dark-haired woman who, Jack realized, looked exactly how he imagined Mia in twenty years, turned from the stove, her face alight with affection. For him.

It made him pause, realize how little affection he had in his life. Now that Mia was cold as ice toward him, there was no one in the world who would greet him like that. No one whose face would light up at his presence.

He looked over at Mia, who was staring down at the limes she was juicing as if they might fly away without all her attention.

How sad was that? Thirty-five years old and he'd burned every bridge that might have led him toward family. Toward belonging to anyone.

Sandra wiped the thick cornmeal goo off her hands onto the tea towel tucked into the tie of her apron, and crossed the kitchen to wrap him in a huge hug, her strong arms a vise around his waist.

She smelled like corn and spice and roses. And he closed his eyes, remembering the thousands of these hugs he'd had while growing up. Every afternoon when he came home from school, Sandra would turn from the dinner she was making and hug him, ask him about his day, bring him a cookie and a glass of milk.

In the aftermath of Victoria's rampages, Sandra would be there, a small shadow offering comfort and a cold cloth. Until he grew such a hard shell he no longer believed he needed such care.

He'd forgotten the good things, pushed them away so as to keep his goals sharp. Those goals became the swords that he used to hack away at the ties that bound him here. But there had been good things at the Rocky M. Mia, her mother and sister had been those good things.

And he'd used those swords to keep them away.

"We're so glad you are safe," Sandra said, looking up at him, her brown eyes warm and worried. "And here!" she cried, "Finally, where you belong."

"Oh, come on, Mom." Lucy, tall and thin, covered in gold bangles and bone necklaces, approached. Her eyes caustic, her smile too bitter for comfort. "Jack belongs to the world."

Sandra stepped aside, and Lucy breezed into her place. Jack tensed, wondering if he was about to get disemboweled.

But Lucy hugged him and leaned up to hiss in his ear, "You're making my sister sad."

"That's not my intention," he said quickly.

She stepped back, assessing him for a moment, and clearly found him lacking. "It never is, is it, you ass," she whispered and moved away.

Her hips bounced to the beat of the music on the radio and she smiled at Jack, as if she hadn't just called him names. "Margarita?" she asked.

"What?" he asked, feeling as if he'd fallen down the rabbit hole. This place had felt more or less like a waiting room the past few weeks. A cafeteria. And suddenly, it felt like a bar.

Or a home.

"It's Saturday," Tim said, as if he'd been waiting his whole life for just such a day. And the way he watched Lucy indicated he'd been waiting for just such a woman. But that was the power of Lucy.

Every woman liked her.

Every man wanted her.

"Sandra's making tamales," Walter said, slicing limes with a steady hand. There was something different about Walter, as if a light had been turned on. The old man's eyes practically glowed and Jack wondered how many margaritas he'd had.

Jack's stomach growled.

"Go," Sandra said, pushing him toward the table, toward Mia where she sat, propped up on pillows. She was spending so much energy pretending she didn't feel him or see him or even notice him, she could have powered the ranch for a month.

He remembered her eyes on him in the shower the other night, the way she'd tracked the touch of his hand on his body. He'd known, watching her, turning the screws with his words, that she'd wished that had been her hand almost as much as he had.

She wasn't immune to him. But she was building that damn tower around herself higher and stronger every day. Keeping herself safe. Keeping him out.

And having Lucy here only helped her cause. Reminded her of all the ways he'd hurt her over the years. And it wasn't as if she needed a whole lot of help in that department.

But maybe having Sandra here helped him.

A few weeks ago he'd felt inert, lost in his own life and directionless. But now, this moment, he felt himself begin to roll toward a destination. Something he wanted.

A home.

Someone to love.

He leaned over the back of her chair and kissed the top of her head. She jerked so hard she nearly broke his nose.

"How are you feeling?" he whispered, his hands on the tender skin of her neck. He could feel her heart beating, the cadence of her breath.

You don't love her, he told himself. Because love wasn't safe. Look at what loving him had brought her. It proved his theory that love brought nothing but pain.

But he wanted her, and right now that was enough. Maybe they could find that happy middle ground. Affection and respect and lust were powerful emotions, strong ones. You could build something with those tools. Something real, like she wanted.

Love was too capricious to be trusted.

He just needed Mia to see that.

"Fine," she said, her voice too loud.

He was making her nervous and he stroked his thumb over her neck, just to be the devil, before dropping into the chair beside her.

Lucy stared at him like a guard dog straining at her chains, but Sandra smiled as she turned back to the tamales.

"You know what you're doing, boy?" Walter whispered from his other side.

"Yes," he whispered back. "Yes, I do."

THIS WAS TURNING into one of those nights Mia used to dream about. Her family, Jack, everyone she loved around a table, laughing, eating mom's homemade tamales.

The right side of her body was electrified, crackling with energy from Jack's closeness.

She'd expected him to be warned off by her family's arrival—good Lord, Lucy was doing her best stern sister act, but Jack seemed impervious. Worse than impervious; he seemed motivated by it. The sterner Lucy got, the cozier Jack got. His leg brushed hers more times than Mia could count. His arm draped across the back of her chair, his thumb brushing her hairline, for half the damn dinner.

And that was bad. It was really bad, but what was killing her was how he seemed to hold court in her home. He told stories, funny ones, scary ones. Some about Oliver that she knew were hard for him, though he didn't once show it. He poured drinks and helped clear dishes.

Even Lucy seemed to have trouble holding on to her grudge.

Lord knows, Mia's grudge had bitten the dust before the second pitcher of margaritas had been made.

"I've always wanted to go to Poland," Lucy said, stretching out her long legs that looked even longer in the leggings she wore under her breezy green tunic. If Mia wore that she'd look like one of Robin Hood's Merry Men. "I've heard there's a beach where amber rolls onto the sand because there's a forest under the Baltic sea."

"A myth," Jack answered.

"No," Lucy moaned. "Don't break my heart."

Mia tried to kick her sister under the table but was too far away and her ankle still hurt.

"The most beautiful amber I've ever seen was in Prague," he said and Lucy leaned forward, entranced because he was speaking to her heart. Her passion.

"The stones were practically red." He shook his head. "I've never seen anything like it."

"What was your favorite place?" Walter asked, and the whole room turned to look at him. The temperature dropped from Jack's side of the table.

"It's a normal question," Walter said, and Mia nodded quickly in agreement.

She felt her heart growing, filling with affection and hope for Walter. Hope that Jack would see the question was sincere. That he would at least consider accepting the olive branch, lame as it may be, that Walter was holding out.

"Prague is lovely," Jack finally said, and Mia took a breath. "Parts of Africa, the Rift Valley, Johannesburg—they're the most beautiful places I've ever seen. The Taj Mahal takes your breath away."

"I'll bet," Sandra said.

"But my favorite place?" Jack asked, slowly turning to face Mia, who was suddenly very uncomfortable, "is Santa Barbara."

Mia felt the world fall away. The room was quiet and heavy with speculation and she didn't care. She didn't care about anything but Jack's chocolate-brown eyes and the peace offering he was holding out to her.

Lucy broke the silence, yammering on about how much she loved the beach town. Mia stared hopelessly at Jack.

Why was he doing this? she wondered. Jack had been so predictable before and now suddenly she didn't know this man in front of her. This man who seduced blatantly and discreetly all at the same time.

"You feeling okay?" he asked, stroking her hand.

She snatched it away.

"Mia," Sandra asked, "do you still have that notebook?"

Her heart sank.

"Mom—" Lucy said, shaking her head. But Mom was choosing to ignore Lucy's not-so-subtle warning and Mia pushed back in her chair, ready to end this night before it fell apart around her.

"Do you still have it?" Sandra asked. "I bet Jack—"

"I'm going to bed," Mia said, getting to her feet. Her back ached from sitting upright so long, and her head pounded with the effort of avoiding embarrassment.

"What notebook?" Jack asked, catching her hand. The calluses on his palm, at the base of his fingers, caught at her skin and she felt the abrasion deep in her core. Her heart.

"She kept a notebook of all the places you went," Sandra explained. "All through college and your internships and research trips. She had—"

"I threw it away," she lied, pulling her hand

back. Jack didn't need any more proof of her childhood crush, her hero worship gone awry.

She'd told him how she felt, as honestly as she could. She'd laid out her heart and he'd offered an experiment in return.

"Good night," she said. She couldn't leave the room fast enough, unable to take a breath until she hit the dark shadows and quiet of the hallway. Damn it. Damn. It.

But she should have known this new version of Jack wouldn't let it go. Wouldn't read the neon signs she was hanging up that she just wanted to be left the hell alone.

No, the new Jack McKibbon would follow. And he did. He caught up with her just past the foyer by the bedrooms, around the corner from the kitchen.

"Mia?"

"Let me go, Jack," she said, crossing the hallway as fast as her wrenched ankle and pounding head would allow.

"I don't think you really want me to," he said, right behind her, so close she could smell the tamale and tequila on his breath.

She paused, something dark and angry

beating at her lips, screaming to get out. But she refrained and kept walking.

Jack's hand touched her elbow and she spun around, smacking at his arm. But still he crowded close, pushing her back until she was up against the wall and every breath she took rubbed her chest against him. Her nipples were hard and painful at the contact.

"Tell me about the notebook, Mia," he almost begged, his eyes searching her face.

"It was nothing. Childish."

"Tell me anyway." He stepped even closer, placing one hand against the wall by her ear. She braced both hands against his chest and shoved.

"Stop crowding me," she ordered.

"Stop running," he said and put his hand right back on the wall. Oh, the contact was killing her. Her body roared to life, a wild rush pulsing through her blood, over her skin. She wanted him. She wanted his taste. His touch.

"Mia." He breathed her name as if he knew. As if he could smell her lust. Her weak-willed desire. He'd primed her for this all through dinner with those long looks, the little touches. He'd been setting down kindling and now he was lighting the fire. "Tell me about the notebook."

She took a deep breath, licked her lips, and a moan rumbled out of his chest, his eyes locked on her mouth. "Tell me about the notebook," he whispered, "or I'm going to screw you against this wall."

Every bone in her body evaporated and she leaned back, her head too heavy to hold. He tilted his pelvis until her hips cushioned his and she gasped at the long, thick press of his erection. Her body burned against his and she arched her hips slightly, pushing into him.

His forehead dropped to hers and she could feel him sweating. Took great pleasure that she could make him sweat.

"You want me to do this to you, don't you?" he whispered, his hips starting a delectable, torturous dance against hers. Back and forth, up and down. He pushed and retreated until she joined him, her hands going to his waist, her fingers twining through his belt loops to keep him close. She angled her hips, and when he next pushed against her, she saw stars.

"Mia," he groaned, licking her neck, her

lips, and she opened her mouth, kissing him with a sudden, wild hunger. She bit his lower lip; he sucked her tongue into his mouth. It was agony, her blood burned, her skin was too tight and Jack wasn't close enough. Not nearly close enough.

He lifted her from the wall, wrapping his arms around her lower back, keeping her feet off the ground. The contact was so delicious she moaned into his mouth. Her arms slid around his neck, her fingers sinking into his thick hair.

He took three steps into her room, and shut the door behind him, holding her weight with one hand and again, just like on that roof, she melted at his strength, at how small and womanly she felt against him.

She felt the floor under her feet, but he didn't let go of her.

"Tell me about the notebook," he whispered against her lips, trailing hot wet kisses across her cheek to her ear. "Mia." He bit the tender lobe. "Tell me."

"I kept a notebook of all the places you went, filled with articles and pictures I found," she said. "So—" She gasped when he slipped his knee between her legs. The friction so good it nearly hurt.

"So?"

"So I knew what you were seeing. And eating. And smelling. So, I could talk to you about it, be there in a way, even when I wasn't."

His kisses stopped, but his thigh was still pressed hard against the screaming junction of her legs. She rocked back and forth.

"What place did you like the best?" he asked, brushing the hair away from her face with both hands.

"Jack," she moaned, beyond pride. She was humping his leg, for crying out loud. "Come on."

"Tell me what place was the most exciting to you." He held her head, compelling her to look at him. He was so serious. His eyes so hot. She forced her hips to stop moving.

"It doesn't matter," she breathed, feeling somehow threatened. Endangered.

"Stop hiding from me, Mia," he demanded, his voice hard, and he slipped his hand between her legs. She shook at the contact, even through her jeans.

Her brain was short-circuiting; she didn't

understand what he was saying, why he wanted her to tell him, or why it seemed like such a bad idea to do it. None of it mattered when his hands pushed inside the waistband of her jeans. His fingers slid across the trembling skin of her belly, the thin elastic at the top of her underwear.

"Tell me," he said. "Where did you want to go?"

"Jack—"

"Tell me and I'll make you come."

Oh, oh, she was dying. She was falling apart. The wild animal of her hunger and her love was taking over.

"Scotland," she said, pressing her head to his shoulder. "Edinburgh."

"My first water summit?"

She nodded. "I liked the castle."

He didn't do anything, his hands were flat against her stomach, not moving. Not keeping his promise.

"Jack," she pleaded, unable to look at him when she was so in need. "Please—"

In a sudden move, he turned and laid her out on the bed. He rolled to her side, keeping one leg hooked over hers, so she was spread out, helpless to his touch.

She closed her eyes, praying for release.

"You have to watch," he whispered, his voice gruff and deep and her eyes popped open. She lifted her head and watched his hand slide into the open vee of her pants.

"You're so wet." He sighed against her ear, using his teeth against her neck. "So hot."

Was she supposed to say something? She hoped not because she was speechless. He shifted down the bed, rearranged his hand so that his thumb found the hard ridge of her clitoris and her body began to hum and shake. She clutched his shoulders, searching for grounding in a world gone white-hot. One finger and then another slid deep inside her and fireworks exploded. She bowed off the bed, her heels digging into the mattress.

His mouth covered hers, swallowing her cries. The screams the whole county would have heard if they'd found their way past his tongue.

He stroked her, softly now, easing her back down. And when the fireworks stopped and her body twitched with random shocks, he smiled, the devil, and whispered, "Once more, Mia. Because you're so damn beautiful."

And it started all over again. But from a

different place, somewhere treacherous and slightly scary, and when she looked into his eyes she couldn't stand it, she had to shut her own.

"Mia," he breathed, chastising her. "Come on."

She shook her head, too far gone to stop, but with just enough awareness to know that if she wanted to survive this, she had to keep something of herself.

She gripped his wrist, grinding herself against his hand, holding him still for her own selfish pleasure and he laughed, dark and hot in her ear.

"That's a girl," he whispered and she exploded again.

Jack removed his hand, his glistening fingers embarrassing her and turning her on at the same time. She lay still, waiting for what was next. What depraved thing Jack had planned for her?

But he rolled away, staring up at the ceiling, his body taut as wire.

"Jack—" She reached out to touch him. The long, hard length of him in his jeans. But he stood up, looking at her on the bed.

"Do you want to go to Edinburgh?" he

asked, and she blinked, not sure she'd heard him correctly.

"What…" Her voice croaked and she tried again. "What are you talking about?"

"You want to go to Edinburgh and I want to take you."

"Now?" she cried. Why weren't they having sex? She didn't have a whole lot of experience, but it seemed like this conversation was a bit of a distraction.

"Summer would be best," he said. "You'd love it. The whole country is like your high pasture."

"Why…" She sat up, but her body wasn't totally on her side and she swayed a little.

"Think about it," he said.

And he left.

CHAPTER FOURTEEN

WALTER WATCHED the coffee pour into the mug and prayed for... He didn't know what exactly, but a prayer right now seemed in order.

"Thank you, Walter." Sandra's voice was low and sweet; she still had that accent. The sound of her and Lucy speaking Spanish filled this old, dark house with color and life. And brought back a lot of good memories.

She stirred some sugar into the coffee, adding cream, and he stood there like a fool, watching her. Remembering all those years he hated himself for noticing his best friend's wife.

"I'm surprised you have decaf," she said, her eyes twinkling.

He'd remembered she drank decaf and had asked Gloria to pick some up with the rest of the groceries. He poured himself a cup and sat down on the chair across from her.

"Look at this place." She sighed. "Hasn't changed at all."

"It's only been five years," he said. "You think we'd redecorate?"

She laughed, the sound like a breeze coming down off the mountains, warm and cool at the same time. "Hasn't changed since I moved into this kitchen thirty years ago."

He looked around, trying to see his home through her eyes. "Hasn't changed practically since I was born." He could feel her watching him and he fought the urge to suck in his stomach. Preen like a peacock.

"How are you feeling, Walter?" she asked. "The Parkinson's disease…"

"Good," he answered and he wasn't lying. Didn't want to lie, not anymore, not to this beautiful woman in front of him. "The medication keeps me on an even keel. I can't do a lot of the stuff I used to—riding a horse is probably beyond me—but I've been helping the men clear the old fire road to the high pasture and it's…it's good."

Sandra's smile was wide, lighting up her face, her round cheeks dimpling. Love lurched in his chest.

"That is very good to hear, Walter," she said. "A man like you should work."

A man like him? What did that mean? He picked apart her words as if they were a riddle.

"Tell me about Los Angeles," he said. "Do you like it?"

She took a deep breath and held it, weighing her answer and he took her hesitation to heart. She didn't like it. He'd never believed she would. Sandra was a woman for open spaces and wild places. The city had to feel like a cage.

"It is very crowded," she said. "And…even working at the church, I am bored. Lucy works such long hours—"

"The jewelry design business," Walter said, and Sandra's eyebrows arched.

"I didn't know you knew," she said.

"I was oblivious to a lot of things," he said. "But your girls were not ones to be ignored."

Sandra liked that. She laughed and laughed and he smiled, pushing his chair closer to the table, as if he could slice right through the wood to be next to her.

She took a sip of coffee and he watched her

long elegant throat through the open collar of her red shirt. They were both sixty-four years old and he felt like a teenager, aware of her, of himself in a way he thought he'd never be again.

He'd felt love for Sandra for a long time.

Desire came as a bit of surprise.

"Where is Victoria?" she asked, staring down at her cup.

"Gone," he said quickly. "After the divorce she moved to Idaho to be with her sister. I haven't heard from her."

She shook her head. "That's no way to end a marriage," she said, and he sat, dumbstruck. Victoria had made Sandra's life miserable five years ago, had made everyone's life miserable for aeons, and she was scolding him for finally divorcing her?

"Marriage is sacred," she said.

"Yeah, that's easy to say when you have a good one," he said. Sandra and A.J.'s marriage had been salt in his wounds.

She nodded, slowly, but he could tell she wasn't agreeing with him. "You gave up a long time ago, Walter," she said.

"I'm sorry," he said, unable to resist sarcasm. "Do you remember my wife?"

"I do," she said, looking him right in the eye, making him feel like a fool. "The woman that hit your son and treated your trusted employees like garbage. I remember her well. Probably better than you, since you weren't around most of the time." She stood up and he realized how badly this was going, how terribly opposite to what he'd dreamed, and he stood up, too.

"I'm sorry, Sandra," he said. "I don't want to fight."

She paused next to him, wrapping a bright blue shawl around her thin shoulders. God, she was lovely.

"You never do," she whispered. "And sometimes…sometimes you need a good fight." She reached up and kissed his cheek, enlivening his old, dried-out body. Then before he could move, she was gone.

Leaving behind the scent of roses and spice and the shame of knowing that even when he thought he was right, he was all wrong.

MIA THREW BLUE'S BRIDLE onto the table in the corner of the tack room, narrowly missing Jack. Which of course had been the plan;

the dream had been beaning him upside the head with a rock.

"Whoa!" he said, turning around. That stupid hat that made him look like the Marlboro Man, but without the cigarettes, sat on his head as if he'd been wearing it every day for the past fifteen years. As if he'd been born wearing it. "Mia, what the hell are you doing out of bed?"

"I'm done with bed," she declared, stepping into the room and kicking the door shut behind her. The aches and pains of her body made her words a lie; she'd be back in her bed soon enough. But not until she had this conversation with Jack.

"What the hell was last night?" she asked, crossing her arms over her chest. It took a lot of courage to do this. She'd stood in her room most of the morning trying to muster up the guts to face this horrifically embarrassing situation head-on.

His smile was slow and knowing, and her body started to simmer.

"I know you're not terribly experienced," he said with a drawl, "but I figure—"

"Stop it, Casanova," she spat. "I'm asking you why. I'm not a toy, Jack."

The smile died. "I know."

"Then why? We agreed on a divorce. You said you were leaving."

"No." He stepped closer. "I said I was leaving after you told me you wouldn't give me a chance—"

"To experiment?" she screeched.

"Yeah." His face got firm, his eyes hard. "I'm sorry my choice of words offended you, Mia. But you have to remember, I don't have all that much experience, either. Now, the way I see it, you're not supposed to be doing heavy work for a while longer, and I'm here for two more weeks until I have to go see the board anyway."

She shook her head. "Forget it, Jack. It won't work."

"Why?"

"Because if you couldn't fall in love with me in thirty years of friendship, or five years of marriage, then why would you fall in love with me in two weeks?"

He stepped closer and then closer again, and she really regretted slamming shut that tack room door. Actually, she really regretted coming out here for this little showdown. She was so weak when it came to Jack. One push, a nudge even, and she'd topple which-ever way he wanted.

"You were right, Mia, I never saw you. Not…this way. Not as a real wife, or a lover. And I'm sorry for the way I hurt you. But listen to me when I say you are not a re-placement for my work. You could never be. You're too…big for that. Too important for that. And I see you now."

"Now?" she asked. "Why is now differ-ent?"

"Because I see everything differently now. My dad, my past, Africa. You. Especially you."

Her fight-or-flight instincts kicked in and she moved backward toward the door, but he grabbed her hand, pulling her close and she had just enough pride to resist.

"I'm looking right at you," he whispered. The world fell away. The tack room. The guys outside. Her injuries, his carelessness. Everything vanished except for Jack McKib-bon looking at her the way she'd always dreamed.

Years too late.

"I'm tough," she whispered, tugging her hand free, wrestling her heart loose. "But not that tough. I can only bend so far. If you hurt me again…I'll break."

She heard Lucy in the barn giving Chris a hard time, and she opened the door to the tack room, letting in cool air and distance. Distance she needed.

"You can stay for two weeks. I do need your help around here, I can't lie. But after that…" She shook her head. "Don't come back."

MIA STOOD NEXT TO LUCY at the horse paddock watching Blue graze on the grass in the south corner.

Well, Mia was watching Blue; Lucy was watching Mia.

"Stop it," Mia whispered.

"I can't," Lucy said, resting her arms on the splintery beams of the fence. "Seriously, honey, you're like a car crash. I just can't look away."

"It's over," she said, as if she'd said, "He's died." Odd that the end of her marriage hurt more now than when she'd brought up the divorce almost three months ago. Then it had been a twinge of pain, some embarrassment that he hadn't fought back. And now that he was fighting back, the end of her marriage felt like a funeral. A death.

"I don't think it was over last night when he followed you to your room and didn't come back," Lucy said, tossing her long, straight black hair over her shoulder. Lucy's hair was like a tame dog compared to Mia's. Always shiny and pretty, it did whatever Lucy wanted. Mia had to muzzle her hair into a ponytail and then a hat just to be presentable. "Honestly, Mia, you should have seen Mom's face. It's like she was counting the minutes until you gave her grandkids."

"There won't be any grandkids. We're getting a divorce."

"Really?" Lucy asked. Mia nodded. Stupid tears welled up in her eyes and she dug her chin into the wood fencepost.

"Then why are you crying?" It should have been obvious, so Mia just sniffed and kept her mouth shut. "You still love him."

"Of course I love him!" she cried. "My God, Lucy, look at the man." She turned, flinging her arm out to where Jack was riding up from the south pasture. She had no idea how she knew he was there, she just did. The same way she knew where north was. He was a part of her compass and she was so scared that when he left, she'd be lost.

"The man looks good in a cowboy hat," Lucy said with a low whistle. "If you go for that kind of thing."

"I'm a rancher," Mia grumbled. "I live for that kind of thing."

"I can see your dilemma."

The silence was soft, comfortable, and Mia realized in a heartbeat how much she missed her sister. How, when Lucy took Mom to L.A., it felt as if part of her had gone missing.

And now that Lucy was back, Mia needed to unload the burden she carried. The baggage she stored and hid away that could no longer be borne alone.

"He's going to go to that university in two weeks and tell them he's responsible for Oliver's death," she blurted.

Lucy hung her head and muttered something under her breath.

"I know it's crazy, and I think *he* knows it's crazy. But I feel bad for him. I feel—"

"Come on now, Mia. How many more years are you going to dedicate to loving a man who doesn't love you back?"

"Ouch, Lucy."

"I know, I'm sorry, I just… I can't watch you put any more time into that man."

"He says he sees me now, really sees me." She looked over and caught her sister's dumbstruck expression. "I think… I mean, I know it sounds desperate, but I think he's changing. I really do."

"But can he change enough?" Lucy asked after a long moment.

Mia's heart pulled and strained like one of the dogs on a leash.

"I don't know," she whispered.

"Well, I know!"

"Stop, please, just stop." Mia looked up at the blue sky, the white clouds. So much beauty and she just didn't care. The world could be gray and it wouldn't make any difference. It would, in fact, only make Jack and his temptation that much brighter.

"Tell me something good," she said, wanting some color in her life. Something to distract her from the fluorescence that was Jack. "Tell me how your business is booming and all the movie stars are wearing your jewelery."

"All the movie stars are wearing my

jewelery because I give it to them," Lucy said, staring down at the dirt.

"Is something wrong?" Mia asked, worried by this cloud on her sister's face.

"Wrong?" Lucy laughed and then shook her head. "It's not exactly what I thought it would be. The designs… Everyone loves the designs."

"Of course they do," Mia said. "They're gorgeous."

"I'm just having trouble with the business part of it." Lucy shrugged. "It's a steep learning curve."

"You'll figure it out," Mia said.

"I always do, don't I?"

Lucy propped her old cowboy boots, which somehow managed to look stylish rather than serviceable, on the bottom rail of the fence and whistled.

Blue came walking over like a lovesick cowboy.

"You haven't lost your touch," Mia said.

"With males of all species?" Lucy asked, her eyes twinkling.

"With horses," Mia said. "Remember when Dad took you to that roundup?"

Lucy smiled and nodded, her eyes far away. "Mom about lost it."

"Well, you were four. But you wouldn't let him leave without you. And I can't blame Mom, those mustang roundups were dangerous."

"Not with Daddy," Lucy said, scratching Blue's nose. "Daddy made everything safe."

Mia nodded in agreement. A truth they'd taken for granted until he died and their world became decidedly unsafe.

"I could never figure out why Victoria thought Mama and Walter had some kind of relationship," Lucy said, shaking her head. "Why on earth would she go after that old drunk when Daddy was around?"

Mia bristled at the name-calling, but she didn't say anything. Growing up, Lucy had never liked Walter. Not that Mia had, either, but taking care of him for the past five years had given her some insight into why Walter did what he did.

Shame and grief could turn a man inside out.

"Mom didn't and wouldn't. Victoria was crazy," Mia said.

"You can say that again. You know," Lucy said, wrapping her arm around Mia's, leading her back toward the house and the bed that waited, "I think it's a good thing that your marriage with Jack is coming to an end."

"You do, do you?"

"You deserve better."

"Like what Mom and Dad had?"

Lucy stopped and turned to face her. "What's wrong with being on your own?" Lucy asked. "There's strength in that."

"And loneliness."

"You think Mom wasn't lonely?" Lucy asked. "Dad worked long hours and Mom had nothing to do but wait for him. Raise his children and keep his meals warm."

"This isn't going to turn into some feminist diatribe, is it?"

"No. Well, maybe. I'm just saying, marriage can be lonely, too."

"You don't have to tell me," Mia snapped. Hadn't she lived in the loneliest marriage for the last five years?

"I know I don't," Lucy said, draping her arm across Mia's shoulders. Lucy took after their father and despite being eighteen months younger, Lucy was a good half foot taller.

"But before you go back to bed to nurse your broken heart, remember that even good marriages are unequal. And as happy as Mom was being married, she's loving her freedom. She's very happy living the bachelor life."

As far as pep talks went, this one was pretty awful, but Mia appreciated the effort. She hugged her sister tight, wishing she could absorb some of her strength and fire. Something to keep her going when everyone left her again. "You're not taking Mom out clubbing, are you?"

"She's taking me out. The woman dances until she drops."

"You're very funny."

"Yes, I am," Lucy said. Mia allowed herself to be pushed back into motion, thinking all the while that her sister was right. Marriages could be unequal and lonely, but she remembered her parents' relationship as a good one. And she wanted one like it for herself.

And if things were different with Jack, maybe she would have had it.

I could still have it, she thought. *If Jack stayed, if I let him stay. If I took the risk he keeps yammering on about...I could have a real marriage. A real husband. I could have the man I love loving me back.*

But the risk was just too much.

"Mia?" Lucy asked, stopping to look her in the eyes. "You okay?"

"My head hurts," Mia said, and it wasn't a lie.

But her heart hurt worse.

MIA WAS KEEPING JACK way past arm's length. He'd barely had a glimpse of her in the past three days. He blamed Lucy. The woman was worse than a guard dog. She was a freaking chastity belt.

"What do you think you're doing?" Lucy had asked around midnight last night when Jack knocked at Mia's door, looking for a second alone with his wife. She was the last person he'd expected to open it.

"You're sleeping with her now?" Jack asked. "Isn't this a little extreme, even for you?"

Lucy narrowed her eyes and lowered her voice. "Haven't you done enough, Jack?"

"No," he said, shaking his head. "I haven't. Because I am trying to keep her."

"Keep her?" Lucy arched a dark eyebrow.

"Like she's a pet?" She started to shut the door and Jack got a hand in to push it open.

"Don't, Lucy, don't do that. I just…I want to try."

"I don't believe you," Lucy said. "And neither does she."

"How am I supposed to convince her if you won't let me talk to her?"

Lucy sighed. "I see your problem," she said.

"Great, then can I talk to her?"

"No," she said, the meanest guard dog to ever wear Betty Boop pajamas. "Go to bed and get over it."

She slammed the door in his face.

Jack was exhausted, frustrated and getting desperate. Mia didn't want him here; she wasn't giving him the chance to fight and he was leaving in a few days to go to the board meeting at the university. His instinct told him to come back, to keep fighting, but he was beginning to wonder if he'd ever win.

Mia had hardened her heart and maybe he needed to respect that. Let them both move on.

The very thought made him sick.

Luckily, there was always plenty of work

to occupy him and the first of the cattle had been moved up to the north pasture, which just left the moms and babies.

He saddled Blue and led the horse out of the barn. He whistled for the dogs, but Daisy and Bear were nowhere to be seen.

"Come on, don't tell me Lucy's got them, too," he muttered, rounding the corner to the front of the barn only to find his father sitting in the old chair Mia had fallen asleep in weeks ago. The dogs sat at his feet, their mottled muzzles on his knees.

"You done spoiling the dogs?" Jack asked. "I got work to do."

"It can keep." Walter stood, a tall man coming all the way to his full height. There was no cane, today. He didn't shake. He didn't tremble. Jack stepped closer and took a whiff of his dad's breath. No booze.

"What's going on?" Jack asked.

Walter licked his lips, a small show of doubt that somehow made Jack nervous. "I want to be a part of your life."

"Excuse me?"

"I want…I want to be a part of your life. I know I've made a lot of mistakes and maybe I can never be your father again. I understand that, but I want… I need to know where you are and what you're doing." Walter didn't look at him, kept his eyes on the dogs, his hands stroking their soft ears.

"I'm trying to herd some cows up to the high pasture," Jack said, deliberately obtuse. This conversation was…unnecessary. Unwanted.

And then he remembered Mia's words, about how he needed to come to grips with his past and his parents in order to have a real relationship. Maybe she was right.

She'd been right about so much.

"Fine," he said. "I'll call you more often."

"You're not staying?"

"Mia's kicking me off the ranch, Dad."

"I want to visit you."

Jack nearly staggered backward.

"I'm not kidding. I want to see where you live."

"Dad, what in the world is bringing this on?"

"I'm fighting for the one damn thing I want, Jack." His burning eyes scorched through Jack's skin, finding dark places, hidden places that hadn't seen light or heat in twenty years. It hurt, and every instinct in him cried out to leave. To find some safety, a rooftop far away. But he grit his teeth and stuck it out, facing it down.

"One thing," his father repeated. "I haven't fought for anything my whole life. I let Victoria bully you, I let her run me away from my own son. I let her drive away the only people who made this house a home."

Walter's eyes were damp, his face was red, emotion rolled off him in waves. More emotion than Jack had ever seen him express.

"Calm down, Dad," he breathed, reaching for Walter, who only shook him off.

"You could learn a lesson from me," Walter said. "You'll die alone, Jack. All alone, if you don't fight for what you want."

"What does this have to do with me?" he asked.

"We're not that different, you and me. The way you treat Mia, have treated her for years—it's the same way I treated you. I ignored you and left you alone, because it hurt to be with you. It hurt to count all the years I let go to waste between us, so I stayed away. Kept my head down and pretended that I wasn't in pain."

Pretended I wasn't in pain.

Those words could have been ripped from Jack's own life. He reeled slightly, trying to make sense of the fact that his father had just bashed him upside the head with the truth.

"We need to fight," Walter said. "If we want a chance to fix things. And that's what I'm doing. Right now. If you were a smart man, which Lord knows you are, you'd do the same. Before it's too late."

Too late, Jack thought, feeling a sudden call to arms. Because failing to fight, or even giving up, leaving when she wanted him to leave and never coming back, only ensured he'd end up like his father.

Alone.

And he didn't want that. Not anymore.

Every day here was another day of his life in the wild. It was as if everything he wanted had broken free of the compartments he used to keep his life simple. Now, it was madness—he was overrun with desire and regret and a thousand wishes that he could make it all right.

"I am fighting," he said, the words making it more true. "For Mia."

Walter's eyes narrowed. "You call what you're doing fighting?"

"I'm trying—"

"You're leaving in three days and every time Lucy looks at you, you cower like a puppy."

Jack opened his mouth to argue, but what could he say? His dad was right.

"Do you love her?" Walter asked.

Jack thought of the way he'd loved Africa at the beginning. How raw it was. How it had tugged at something primal and true, uncomplicated and pure, in his gut. The way he'd stepped foot on that soil and felt useful in a way he never had before. Vital. The people there who'd shown him every single moment what it meant to be gracious and joyful, not that he ever seemed to practice that.

But he wanted to. And that was new.

He thought of the way he'd loved his work. How it had felt at the beginning, as though it was just him against the problems. And how those problems had engaged him and absorbed him. Until he didn't know who he was without the work. Until he could push away all those things in his life that weren't easily solved.

Those emotions seemed so small when it came to Mia.

He'd thought that love was a separate entity. Something he could label, hold in the palm of his hand and quantify, but suddenly he realized it was bigger than that. It was all-encompassing.

At this moment, science failed him and he had no frame of reference for what he felt for Mia. It was as if his feelings for her were the invisible trusses, beams and joists for everything in his life.

Mia made his feelings for those other things possible. Her faith in him, her belief that he could accomplish what he set out for, made it possible to believe in himself.

Her integrity and passion for her own work inspired a passion for his.

She had always anchored him; no matter where he'd been in the world, he'd always come back to her. Because his home wasn't the Rocky M, or his condo in San Luis Obispo. It wasn't even his work. Or Africa.

Mia was his home.

And now that he was finally seeing his past for what it was—and himself for who he was—he understood that she'd owned his heart all these years.

"Yeah," he said, feeling like a man who'd been blinded by a solar eclipse. He loved Mia. Loved her so much and so long it had become a part of his landscape. His own body. He just hadn't recognized it until now. "I do."

Walter smiled, his face lighting up for a bright second, and Jack felt hurtled in time. He stood there like a kid filled with all the hero worship a son should have for his old man, before tarnish ruined everything. And Jack wanted to hold on to that sweetness. The innocence. He wanted to forget the abuse and the neglect. The way it seemed his father turned his back on him.

And he wanted to remember the good things. The good times.

The bitter knot of anger and resentment shifted sideways in his chest, opening up some new place, a hidden chamber with light and a view.

Maybe this was forgiveness?

He wished Mia was here. She would tell him for sure.

"Well," Walter said. "I'm just letting you

know. I expect you to keep in touch better than you have been. A card now and again—"

"You want to come with me?" Jack asked. "I'm moving heifers up the fire road."

Walter's eyes dimmed and he ran a wrinkled hand over his barrel chest. "Can't ride, son."

"We'll take the truck," he said, not sure why he was pursuing this. "The dogs can do most of the work."

Bear barked at the news; Daisy scratched her ear.

Dad watched him, as if he knew that Jack wasn't convinced. That half of him wished he could swallow back the words.

"Sounds good," Walter said, clapping Jack on the shoulder, leading the way to Mia's beat-up truck.

Jack lingered for a second, wondering how in a conversation about fighting for what you want, he ended up riding herd with his dad for the first time in fifteen years.

CHAPTER FIFTEEN

JACK WAS LEAVING in two days. It was as if the calendar was embedded in her heart. Her head.

She rolled over and looked at her sister, sleeping next to her in the bed because there were no other rooms. Lucy snored. Her stylish, composed sister snored like a trucker. And slept like the dead. If it weren't for the snoring, Mia might be concerned.

Lucy wouldn't hear Mia if she eased out of bed and snuck across the room. The door barely creaked anymore. She could be in Jack's room, sliding under the covers, up against all that blanket-warmed bare skin and Lucy wouldn't even stir.

But she didn't do it.

You're a chicken, she told herself. *A coward. You're letting fear rule your life.*

She flopped onto her back.

He was changing, she could see it. But was

it enough? Truly? Enough to risk her heart again? Every time she'd gone to one of those functions with him and she'd seen him light up at the sight of her, her heart had exploded with joy. But by the end of the night he'd be deep in conversation with Oliver about the next project and she'd once again be an afterthought.

He was focused on her now, and it was a heady delight.

But what happened when his attention wandered, back to his work, his old life, some new project? She'd be an afterthought again. And not even she was strong enough for that.

She wished she could look into his eyes and see the truth. The future.

But there was no guarantee, and if she was going to be honest with herself, she knew that was what she needed. Without it, she had to let him go. She had to. But could she really let him go without touching him one last time? Kissing him?

It seemed impossible.

She had the rest of her life to be alone and only a few more chances to be Jack's wife.

She slipped out of the bed, glancing back

at Lucy to be sure she hadn't woken, then crept out of the room. It was just past dawn. Jack might be awake, and if she was lucky she'd get him before he left his bed.

Before she'd taken more than two steps into the hallway, Walter's door opened and she froze like a thief.

Walter was fully dressed for a day of work. A denim shirt rolled up over muscular arms, tucked into a pair of dark brown canvas pants.

"What are you doing?" she asked as if he'd stepped out of his room in a clown costume.

"Branding," he said.

"So soon?" she cried. She figured that would be the first thing she'd organize once she was back full steam.

"Wanted to get it done before I left," Jack said and she turned. She hadn't heard his door open. He stood in the new dawn sunshine in hard-worn blue jeans and a black long-sleeved T-shirt. Her heart pounded in her chest, her mouth went dry and the grief, the grief that buzzed around her head like a fly waiting to land, was deafening.

"You don't have to do that," she said.

He watched her for a long time, long enough that Walter grumbled something about breakfast and headed down the hallway toward the kitchen.

"You won't let me stay," he said. "You won't let me come back. You won't let me help you."

"I don't need your guilt or your charity," she said, raising her chin.

He stepped out into the hallway, taking up too much space. Too much air. "It's not guilt," he said. "Would you believe I like the work?"

"No."

His smile was sharp. "Well, I do."

"What are you doing with Walter?" she asked.

Jack shrugged and pulled his door shut. "He misses the work, and it's easy enough to drive him up to the pasture. Let him hang out."

"Hang out?" Mia asked, wondered if the whole world was upside down or just this ranch. "With your father? The man you haven't talked to in years?"

"You told me I needed to deal with my past and that's what I'm doing."

Flabbergasted, all she could do was nod. "How…how is that going?"

His gaze lifted over Mia's head to the kitchen at the end of the hallway, where they could hear Walter talking to Sandra. "Better than I thought it would. It's still not perfect, but it's better."

Affection and pride flooded her chest. "I'm so glad."

"What I'm wondering," he said, leaning closer. He tilted his head, smiling at her like a wolf. "Is what you're doing outside my door at dawn."

"It doesn't matter now, does it?" she asked, feeling peevish and confused. "You're off to brand."

His laugh rang bells all over her body. "It matters, Mia." He touched her cheek, her lip. "I'll see you tonight," he murmured and left her stewing in her own frustration.

JACK AND THE GUYS came in later than usual, but they had the easygoing laughs of men who'd finished a job.

"You're kidding," she said, when Chris told her the work was done. "All of them are branded?"

"I hired two seasonal hands," Chris said. The guys all filed into the room and sat down at the big table. Sandra had made spaghetti with meatballs and the men dug in as if they hadn't eaten in weeks. They'd eaten that way every night since Sandra had been back. Even Chris seemed to have put on weight.

And Mom watched from the stove, a smile on her face.

"On whose authority?" Mia cried.

"Mine," Jack said, grabbing an apple from a bowl on the counter that had sat empty for five years. "It's my money, after all."

She shook her head, anger and purpose filling her. She'd been an outcast from her life, from her work long enough. "No more bed rest," she snapped. "This is ridiculous."

"I agree," Jack said, taking a giant bite of the bright red fruit, juice dripping down his chin. He looked so earthy, so raw, it felt erotic just to look at him, to stand here and watch him eat.

She could barely blink in fear of missing something.

"Sandra?" he said. "You got that box ready?"

"Here you go." Sandra lifted a big box up

onto the counter. "Try to have her home by midnight or she'll turn into a pumpkin."

"What the hell is going on?" Mia demanded.

"I'm taking you on a picnic," he said.

A picnic? Her breath shook in her chest, her heart missed a beat.

"Mom, what did you do?" Lucy asked from behind her. Mia couldn't turn; she was riveted by Jack.

"I packed up some fried chicken and a couple of brownies for my daughter and her husband," Sandra said, the word *husband* laced with dynamite.

"Sounds wonderful, Sandra," Jack said with a charming smile and Mom blushed.

"We're here to help Mia," Lucy said. But it all seemed so far away to Mia. The only thing she cared about, the thing she could touch, was Jack.

"Stay out of this, Lucy," Jack said. "This is between me and my wife."

My wife? Was this really happening?

"Mia," Lucy said, coming to stand beside her, tugging her hand. "This isn't a good idea."

"Lucy. Stop." Walter's voice boomed

through the big room and everyone froze. Except Lucy, who whirled on the old man.

"Who the hell are you to tell me what to do?" Lucy asked.

Sandra threw her dish towel over her shoulder and stepped out from behind the stove into the fray—and still, Mia could not look away from Jack.

"A picnic," he whispered, his eyes twinkling, his lips wet with juice. "Away from the maddening crowd."

Mia knew it was a bad idea, just like she'd known going up on that roof in Santa Barbara had been a bad idea, but she was tired of resisting. Tired of being safe in her misery and loneliness. When Jack left—and he would—she wanted memories. She wanted something real to hold on to.

"Let's go," she said.

"THE ROOF of the high school?" she asked, a half hour later, staring up at the old fire escape that led to the air-conditioning unit over the cafeteria.

"Only the finest," Jack said, tucking Sandra's picnic dinner into the old beat-up knapsack he'd brought along. He still couldn't quite believe she'd come with him. After days of pushing him away, that she was here seemed like a miracle.

A miracle he planned on taking full advantage of.

"You first," he said, bowing slightly as if escorting her to the best seat in the house.

She shot him a wry look. "Don't stare at my butt," she said, starting up the ladder.

"Wouldn't dream of it," he said, staring at her butt. Good Lord, the woman's curves had curves.

They climbed up the ladder to the top of the air-conditioning unit and then chinned up onto the flat roof over the main part of the school.

She didn't need his help, as ready as he was to give her a boost. Mia Alatore got where she wanted to go all by herself, and it was one of the things he most admired about her.

He wondered if she knew that.

How would she? he asked himself. *You never bothered to tell her.*

Calling a woman tough was hardly a love song. And Mia deserved whatever love songs he could give her.

"Seems like other people have found your hiding spot," she said, kicking aside beer bottles and empty cans of spray paint. A filthy mattress crouched in the dark corner next to a big vent.

"They need to take down that ladder," he said, saddened to see his old refuge so misused. "It's too damn easy to get up here."

"The view is still the same," Mia said, looking out at the mountains, bathed in pink light from the setting sun. The small town of Wassau spread out in front of them for a couple of blocks in either direction.

A kingdom of split-level ranch houses and pickup trucks.

"I feel like a queen up here," she said, laughing. She tucked her hands into the pockets of the red zip-up sweatshirt she wore and tilted her head back to the breeze.

How was it that she was the most beautiful woman he'd ever seen? Dressed in a sweatshirt and cowboy boots, she beat every other woman by a mile.

"I was more inclined to a god on Mount Olympus," he said, and she shot him a dubious look over her shoulder. A look that sent arrows through his body. His heart.

"You were such a nerd," she groused.

"I don't know." He shrugged off the backpack and opened it up, pulling out a blanket and some food. He wished he had wine, but he'd have to make do with two bottles of water. "Pretending to be a god makes sense for a kid who felt like he had no control in his life."

"Listen to you," she said. "All Oprah about your childhood."

Jack laughed. "I wouldn't go that far, but... you were right. I'm never going to have a real relationship with anyone if I kept pushing them away or leaving them."

The atmosphere on the roof changed and he could feel Mia's anxiety, see it in the set of her shoulders under that red sweatshirt.

It was now or never and as much as he wished he had more than an apple in his nervous stomach, as intricate a seduction as he'd had planned, he knew he couldn't let this moment go by. He'd let too many moments go by, blind to them.

"I'm coming back to the ranch," he said. "After the meeting with the university, I'm coming back."

Mia hung her head and his heart ached for

her, it really did, but he wasn't going to be pushed around by her fears anymore.

"It's my home, Mia."

"For how long?" she asked.

"For as long as you'll have me." These past few days with his father had started to unravel the mess of his childhood.

The things he'd thought were real—that his father didn't love him, that his mother's hate and rage were somehow his fault—he now knew were false.

Except for Mia. Mia had always been real. Mia was joy in a world of cold science.

"I love you," he said, and she jerked as if he'd shot her.

But she didn't turn.

"I put my whole life in compartments," he said, keeping his distance, knowing if he touched her she'd run. So he stood back and hoped his words would do the job. "I had my work. I had the past. I had you. And I kept everything separate. Simple. I didn't think about the past or you when I thought about work and so, I let work take over."

"Because it was easier," she said.

"Yes," he agreed, watching her for clues. But she was unreadable. A stone face. And he wanted to feel hope, joy even that he'd told her how he felt. That he'd loosened some of the chains of his past, but her stoicism wouldn't allow it.

Panic started a drumbeat in his head.

"But I want it all," he said, pushing on anyway. "I want a full life. A real life. I want you and my work to occupy the same place. To coexist."

"How can we if your work is all over the world?"

"I don't know what my work is going to be, Mia. Maybe I'll stay here and fix irrigation systems."

She scoffed. "Like that will make you happy."

"You make me happy." And then, because he couldn't not touch her any longer, he curled his hand over her shoulder, feeling her heat and bone and muscle. But he felt none of her heart. None of her love.

She was closed off to him.

"You don't believe me." It wasn't a question. "I'm sorry I hurt you," he said. "I'm sorry I left. Trust me when I tell you I didn't know what I was leaving behind. I didn't know I was leaving the better part of myself, the laughter and the love. I didn't know I was leaving behind my best friend and my family."

She stared up at him, dry-eyed and doubtful.

"I'll prove it," he said, grabbing hold of the challenge with both hands. He pulled off her hat tossed it to the ground at their feet. Slowly and gently he untangled the ponytail from the nape of her neck. The breeze picked up her hair, blew it around her head. A lusty contradiction to the stone-cold look in her eye.

"You don't scare me," he whispered. She thrilled him. Excited him. And if his words didn't get the job done, he had other ways to convince her.

MIA WAS A LAMB headed to slaughter and she wouldn't have it any other way.

Jack took his time, breathing whisper-thin words against her skin like *love* and *home*. Words that wound around her like a spell.

Don't believe, she warned herself.

And then he kissed her and she couldn't help it. This was Jack holding her. Jack, her husband, telling her he loved her. How could she not at least hope? How could she pretend to be unmoved?

He didn't play games, held the back of her head and opened his mouth over hers. It was lush and exciting. Wet and all-consuming. A thousand never-ending kisses.

Her body turned to mist and she lost all boundaries, all sense of herself as something other than him. Other than raw sensation. She opened herself up and took everything he gave her. She had no protection, just desire and the man she loved.

She moaned and wrapped her arms around his waist, pulling herself to him, angry when it didn't seem like enough.

"Mia—"

"Shut up," she muttered, unzipping her jacket and tossing it over her shoulder. Closer. She wanted to be closer to him.

His chuckle rumbled against her chest and she didn't appreciate him laughing at her. She dropped her hand to his belt buckle and his laughter died on a cough. His wiry strength was taut, expectant, waiting for her next move and she liked that. She really liked that.

Slowly, carefully, she ran her hands over the

jeans below his belt, feeling the hard length of him beneath the metal and denim.

His groan threw gasoline on the fire burning in her body. Her nipples hardened so fast they hurt and the ache between her legs grew, spreading through her body.

He'd spread out a blanket and she tucked her fingers inside the waistband of his jeans and pulled him toward it, aglow in the last of the sunset.

His shirt rode up and under her fingers she felt the soft tenderness of his belly. The white-hot heat of his skin. She pushed her fingers deeper and felt the wiry curls of the hair that grew there.

It wasn't enough; the teasing, fleeting sensations weren't enough to satisfy her suddenly voracious curiosity. And appetite.

She leaned up on tiptoe and kissed him while her fingers undid his belt. His palms slid over her hips, grabbing her ass with both hands, squeezing and pulling her close. She lost focus for a moment, groaning into his mouth, pressing her aching breasts against his chest, searching for someplace to put this desire.

She wanted him in her hands. Her mouth.

She wanted to suck on him. Taste him on her tongue. Feel him against her lips.

She'd never done this. Not really. And she planned to take her time. She planned to master the skill of pleasing her husband, right now.

Jack muttered something dark and dirty into her mouth and she wanted to laugh with wicked delight.

Finally, her awkward fingers got rid of the belt and the button and zipper of his jeans and she slid her hands into his pants.

His erection, hot and smooth, leaped into her fingers and she curled her palm around him.

He hissed, his hips jerking against hers.

"Mia, baby, listen, I love this, but it's…it's been a long time."

She didn't say anything. Wasn't about to let him off the hook. She had a plan, damn it, and he wasn't going to make a mess of this the way he had her life.

A gentle push and he was on his back on the blanket. His shirt had been pulled up and she saw the muscles of his stomach, the tip of his erection. His pants were stubborn, but she tugged them down past his hips, revealing the full length of him. The dark, coarse hair.

She'd seen men who weren't her husband, of course. Well, just Bill Winters. But this was her husband, and love made him beautiful, so much more than his body and his skin and hair.

"Men like this," she said, though she wasn't sure why. Doubts, maybe. She was, after all, a thirty-year-old almost virgin.

"If you're talking about what I think you're talking about…yes, they do."

She ran her fingers over him, feeling the veins that pulsed just beneath the skin. His hips lifted off the ground and his legs shifted, bumping into her knees where she knelt.

His reaction excited her and she gripped him in her hand, ran her thumb over his tip, smearing the thick liquid she found there. She brought her thumb to her lips and while he watched, panting through open lips, she licked it off.

"Mia," he groaned.

Yes, she thought, heat and desire pulsing through her. *I like this.*

She leaned over him, licked him from base to tip and he groaned, twitching beneath her.

She sucked him into her mouth, loving the masculine scent of him and he yelled, fisting his hands into her hair, showing her what he wanted, how fast, how hard.

He praised her, his words raunchy and rough, and she wanted to laugh with delight. With how damn alive she felt. How connected to him and to her own womanhood. Her own power.

She used her hands, stroking him against the rhythm of her mouth, and he really seemed to like that. So she did it some more.

Until he pulled her away, his hands clumsy. His face was stony. She watched him, spellbound, her body aching, as he kicked off the rest of his clothes and turned toward her—a different Jack.

A Jack with all that urbane intelligence turned off. A Jack without the distance his brain put between himself and the rest of the world.

He was focused—a hundred percent—on her.

He tore off her pants, pushed down her underwear, and the violence was exhilarating. She'd driven him to this place, where he barely had control. Where that powerful brain of his was negated by his physical needs.

He spread her legs and rolled on top of her. He eased his fingers between them and she knew he was gauging her readiness.

She was more than ready.

When his fingers touched the wet heat of her, he kissed her. Hard.

He shifted again and when he thrust inside her, she screamed in welcome. The sound tearing out of some hidden place inside her. She relished his lack of control, but in truth, was scared of losing her own.

She struggled against him for a second, trying to find space for herself, the distance she needed to keep herself safe.

"No, Mia," he said, forcing her to look at him. He pushed himself high and hard and she gasped, choking on pleasure. "Don't pull away. Not now."

"Jack—"

"This is us. Right here. Right now," he said, his eyes boring into hers as he started to move. It was so beautiful she nearly cried.

Us, she thought, matching his rhythm, his violence.

Distance, safety? The need was gone, the urge erased.

He bent his head, found her nipple with his mouth, lips and tongue. He thrust and kissed and sucked, driving her somewhere she'd never been. Didn't even know existed.

She bit her lip against a thousand screams. She closed her mouth against the *I love you* and the *I need you and please, please don't leave me* that clawed to be free.

Pleasure, thick and heady, rolled through her, gathering speed, pulling at every cell. For a second she was scared, scared of letting go quite this much, but then Jack slid his fingers through hers and buried his face in her neck.

"I love you," he whispered and she exploded.

CHAPTER SIXTEEN

THE HOUSE WAS QUIET, but Walter knew Sandra wasn't sleeping. He'd heard her in the kitchen, her soft footfalls leading to the living room.

He waited a few moments and then went to find her.

"Walter?" Her voice was a sweet caress.

Fight for what you want, he told himself.

"Evening, Sandra," he said.

"What's got you wandering around so late?"

"I was…" He stopped the lie on his lips.

Fight, he told himself, but he didn't know exactly how to do that. He figured he'd do what he did with Jack. He'd start with the truth.

"I was looking for you," he said.

His eyes adjusted to the light and he saw her curled up in the couch, wrapped in that blue shawl. She looked like a robin's egg and he wanted to pick her up, hold her in his arms.

"Well, you found me," she said and he heard something different in her voice, something that turned that smile of hers into a lie. Sadness.

She'd been sitting here crying.

"Are you all right?" he asked, sitting down next to her, so aware of her leg inches away from his.

"I am, Walter," she said, wiping at her eyes. "I am fine. I think, maybe, being in this house is harder than I thought it would be."

His heart tripped and his "fight for what you want" pep talk died a scared little death.

"You miss your husband," he whispered.

"I do." Her voice cracked. "I do." She took a deep breath and began to stand up. "I should go," she said, but he put his hand on her arm, feeling the warmth of her skin under the shawl. He wanted to hug her, pull her into his arms, rub his hands down the elegant curve of her back—give and take whatever comfort they could offer each other.

He'd been frozen for so long, since way before Jack was even born.

"Tell me what's wrong, Sandra," he pleaded, but she shook her head, the tension ratcheting up until it felt as though the whole roof might blow off.

"Please," he whispered, wanting to take away her pain.

"I'm so mad!" she yelled and he was so shocked he reached for her, but she slapped at his hand and the eyes she turned on him were livid. "I'm so mad at you," she hissed.

"Me?"

"This was my home. I cared for it. I cared for every person here and you let that woman—" She stopped, shaking her head, gathering herself together. "I'm sorry, Walter. It's been a long night and I think I should just go."

"I think you should say what you need to say," he told her, seeing the undeniable need in her. What he had to tell her seemed useless in front of all her suppressed feelings. He felt like a fool, coming in here with plans to unburden his pathetic heart, while she stewed in an anger he'd never seen.

She clenched the ends of that shawl in

bone-white fists. "I'm angry that you let that woman ruin this home, your family, all because you were a coward."

He flinched, but stayed silent. Sandra had a good head of steam on and showed no sign of stopping.

"A.J. was your best friend, he worked this land beside you and you let his family get pushed out of the only home we'd ever known, weeks after his death, before we even had a stone on his grave."

"I'm so sorry—"

"I know you are, Walter. You're a sorry man. And I thought I could come back here and feel nothing, but I have twenty-five years of living in these walls and if I'd had my way I would have died here and been buried right beside my husband. And I was robbed of that."

More apologies rose to his lips, but he kept quiet, his heart beating a ragged rhythm in his chest.

"Lucy and I will be leaving soon," she said.

"You don't have to," he said quickly. "You can stay. I...I would like you to stay."

She watched him a long time and finally

shook her head. "No," she said. "It's too late. Lucy's business is in L.A., and that's where we belong."

He wanted to argue with her—hell, any fool could see she wanted to stay here. But it wasn't his place.

"Good night, Walter," she breathed and left, silently crossing the living room.

When she was gone and the shadows turned from purple to black, he took a deep breath.

"I love you," he whispered, letting loose the words he'd come into the room to say. "I've always loved you."

Silence answered him, the silence of an almost empty house, like a cave with nothing but cobwebs and echoes. Ghosts of a life that might have been.

"I need a drink," he muttered and went in search of his bottle.

MIA WAS A COUNTRY MUSIC SONG brought to life. Curled up against her husband on the bench seat of her pickup. The sweet smell of spring turning to summer rolling in through the open windows.

All they needed was one of the dogs. Maybe a kid.

The thought was bittersweet and she pushed it away before it could grow into a wish.

"Why did your dad marry your mother?" she asked, and Jack shook his head.

"We haven't talked about it," he said. "Frankly, I don't want to bring it up."

Mia hummed in response. Unable to help herself, she tilted her nose closer to his chest, just so she could smell him. Laundry soap and hard work and just a little bit of sex.

"Are you sniffing me?"

"Yep. You smell good. Like sex."

Jack's chuckle rumbled under her ear and she didn't know when she'd ever felt this happy. This…complete.

"I'm leaving day after tomorrow," he said.

Great, she thought, leaning away from the magnetic heat of the man she loved. Good feeling gone.

He braked and threw the truck into Park. The lights from the ranch were just around the corner and Mia wished she were there right now so she could hide out in her room and avoid this goodbye. She'd had enough of them. Wasn't strong enough to do it again, with a brave smile and dry eyes.

Part of her was dying and she didn't want to pretend otherwise.

"Come with me," he said, shocking her. "I want you to come. I meant what I said on that roof. I love you, Mia." She opened her mouth, but nothing but a choked gasp came out. "It's only a few days. With branding done, Chris and the boys can handle—"

"Okay," she breathed. She knew what she was doing, the great gamble she was taking against terrible odds, but she couldn't help it. Her better judgment was in some kind sex-sated coma and her heart was running the show.

"Okay?" he repeated, as surprised as she was that she'd agreed. She nodded, unable to stop the smile, the strange giggle that erupted from all her happy places. He hauled her into his arms. "Oh, my God, Mia," he breathed into her hair. "Thank you. Thank you so much, I know how hard—"

"We both do," she said, putting her hands over his mouth before he woke up her better judgment. "Let's leave it at that."

"You won't be sorry," he said, kissing her lips, her cheeks. "I promise you, you won't be sorry."

I hope not, she thought. *I really hope not.*

"You're going with him?" Lucy asked the next morning, standing in Mia's bedroom door like a Roman guard. All she was missing was a sword and shield. "Tell me you're joking."

"She is trying to make her marriage work," Sandra said. Mom, opposite of Lucy, was helping her pack. No doubt putting baby prayers all over Mia's clothes.

"She is trying to break her own heart. Again." Lucy stepped into the bedroom, shutting the door behind her.

"I think…" Mia took a deep breath and took the black dress Lucy had loaned her for the Santa Barbara trip out of her closet. "I think it's going to be okay and I know you just want the best for me, Lucy. But I think…I think Jack is the best for me."

"Listen to you," Lucy said. "You're not even sure yourself and you're trying to convince me?"

Mia stared at her sister for a long time. "I know it seems crazy," she whispered.

"Totally loco," Lucy agreed.

"But…I can't not do it," she said. "I can't let him go without trying everything I can to make my marriage work."

"That's my girl," Sandra said, taking the dress from Mia's hands. "Marriage takes effort. Relationships take effort. Your sister doesn't know this because she is too busy to date."

"Oh, ho!" Mia laughed and Lucy groaned. "Score one for Mom."

"Fine," Lucy said. "But if you're going away for the weekend, you're not taking these." Lucy reached into Mia's suitcase and pulled out a handful of cotton underwear.

"Hey!" Mia said, trying to grab them back.

"Your sister is right. That underwear does not belong on a weekend with your husband," Sandra said, and Lucy and Mia shared a quick horrified expression. "What?" Sandra asked, a vixen's smile on her lips. "Your father was a happily married man for thirty-six years and it wasn't because I'm a good cook."

Lucy dug through Mia's drawers for the

silk and lace scraps that she bought her every year for her birthday.

"Now," Sandra said, zipping up the packed bag. "Since you are back on your feet and everything seems to be in hand here, I think it's time Lucy and I headed home."

"What?" Mia asked.

"Yeah, what?" Lucy seconded.

"We are not needed here," Sandra said with a shrug.

"You're kidding, right?" Mia asked, wondering why her mother was saying this. "You've made this house a home again, Mom. Honestly, you can't leave now."

"But Lucy's work—"

"Can keep," Lucy said, and Mia turned to her sister, surprised to hear her volunteer to stay. "It can," Lucy said. "And the truth is, I want to be here when you get back. I want to see for myself that you're okay."

"I'll be fine," Mia said, stroking her sister's shoulder. "But thank you."

Sandra was shaking her head. "I really think it's time."

"Mom," Mia said, "I know Walter seems all right now, but two months ago the man could barely walk. I would feel a lot better leaving for a few days if I knew someone was here to watch him."

"I am not that man's nursemaid," Sandra said with more venom than Mia had heard from her mother in years.

She shot a quick glance at her sister, who seemed just as baffled at their mother's sudden adamant desire to leave.

"I know you're not and I wouldn't dream of asking you to be. The truth is, he'll probably be fine, but I would feel better knowing you were here. To help if it was needed."

Mom could never resist a call to help, but still she seemed reluctant, so Mia pulled out the big guns.

"For me."

Sandra groaned and muttered something in Spanish that Mia couldn't quite hear.

"She just put double the baby-making curses on you," Lucy whispered.

"They are prayers," Sandra said, wrapping her arms around her girls. Mia dove into the hug, hauling her family against her.

"Fine," Sandra whispered. "We'll stay until you come back, but then we leave."

"Okay," Mia agreed.

The world was different today. Colored

in shades of hope and happiness, and she couldn't find it in herself to doubt. It seemed like sacrilege in the face of all this love.

So she didn't doubt. She believed, with her whole heart, that her life was beginning anew.

CHAPTER SEVENTEEN

THE NEXT DAY, a thick tension surrounded Jack. Standing next to him made Mia feel as if she was in quicksand up to her neck. She couldn't even breathe as they stopped in front of the conference room doors.

"It's going to be okay," she said, trying to sound optimistic.

He nodded stiffly, running a hand down his tie. "It's just a formality," he said. "I've already resigned."

She didn't say anything; the argument over his resignation had nearly ruined the drive from the ranch. She felt he was making a decision based on grief and in a few years' time, he'd regret it. He'd wish for his old life back.

"Have some faith in me, Mia," he'd said. "I know my own mind."

It had been an inauspicious beginning to a weekend that had only gone downhill.

Dinner last night had been stilted. In a college town like San Luis Obispo, everyone knew everyone. The second she and Jack sat down to eat, it seemed as though everyone in town came by to see how he was doing and to express their condolences over Oliver.

Jack had sat there with so much grief in his face she'd had to go to the bathroom to dry her eyes.

He'd dropped her back at his apartment, and gone to the university to take care of some loose ends. His condo was a two-bedroom with a beautiful view of the mountains and almost totally devoid of any sign of life, much less personality.

Looking in the cupboard at his two coffee cups and three plates, she started to believe that maybe he did know his own mind. Maybe he was ready to leave this empty life he lived behind.

That sense was reinforced when he came home last night, sliding into his king-size bed and holding her so tight she couldn't tell his heartbeat from hers.

"I'm sorry," he'd whispered. "I've been so distant. This is harder than I thought."

"It's okay," she'd said, rolling over in his

arms, cupping his face in her hands. She didn't believe her own assurances, but she wanted him to believe it.

And now, in front of the conference room doors, Jack looked like a man heading toward the hangman's noose.

"You don't still blame yourself, do you?" she asked, smoothing down the worst of his haywire hair.

She should have given him a haircut before they left the ranch.

"It's not that simple, Mia," he said, moving away from her touch. She tried not to take it personally, but everything was so screwed up. Jack was living in his head again and she couldn't figure out how to reach him. "I know I'm not the reason they're dead, but I would feel a whole lot better if I had done everything in my power…" He shook his head, his breath shaking when he exhaled. "Christ, if I had just done my job. Maybe…"

Her heart ached for him and as much as she wanted to touch him, she couldn't. Between the tension and his mood, the arguments they'd already had about this, she didn't know how to navigate this situation.

Doubt, whisper-thin but poisonous, crept in along the seams of her belief. Her love.

You don't fit in here, doubt said. *His world has no room for you.*

But he was leaving this world behind, she reminded herself, throwing her shoulders back in the black dress. A dress that was totally inappropriate, she knew, but it was the only slightly nice thing she had. It didn't feel right to wear jeans and cowboy boots and that was all she owned.

"Thank you for being here," he whispered, lifting her hand and kissing her fingers, breathing warmth onto her palm. "I don't know if I could do this without you."

She kissed his ear. "I'm glad to be here," she said, pushing the doubts aside. "Should I go in with you?"

He shook his head. "You can wait at the end of the hallway," he said. "There's a faculty lounge there. Coffee and stuff."

She nodded, wishing she could make a joke or something, anything to lighten the mood, but she felt so ill-equipped. It was tough not to wish they were back on the ranch.

He kissed her hard on the mouth and then opened the door.

Sunlight flooded the hallway from the floor-to-ceiling windows in the conference room, and she got a quick look at a bunch of men in suits before Jack slipped in, shutting the door behind him.

Well, she thought, staring at the dark wood door. *I guess now I wait.*

But she sure as hell wasn't going to wait in the killer shoes she was wearing. She slipped them off with a sigh of ecstatic relief before heading down the hallway toward the lounge.

The room was cheerful, with yellow walls, a stainless-steel fridge and large windows that looked out over the mountains and the busy quad in the center of campus. A white counter crowded with small appliances ran along a far wall and the rest of the room was filled with an old couch and a couple of empty chairs and tables.

The coffee smelled old but strong, and she walked across the cool tile toward a cupboard looking for a mug.

She found about thirty of them and chose one with a horse on it. The coffee was as bad as it smelled, but she took the full cup and headed over to the fridge looking for milk.

Beside the fridge was a bulletin board filled with press clippings. All about Jack.

Pictures of Jack and Oliver shaking hands with the president. And Matt Damon. Surrounded by the smiling faces of a dozen children.

Headlines screamed: Professor Brings Water And New Life To Village. Scientists Changing the World One Well At A Time. Cal Poly Faculty Shortlisted For Humanitarian Award. President Obama Asks To Meet Faculty.

Two people walked in and Mia jumped, coffee splashing down the front of her dress.

"Crap," she muttered, pulling the soaked fabric away from her chest.

"Are you…lost?" the woman asked, and Mia looked down at herself, barefoot and wearing a cocktail dress. On a Monday morning.

Mia scrambled into her shoes.

"No, no, I'm Mia Alatore—I'm Jack McKibbon's wife."

"Oh!" The woman smiled and reached out to shake her hand. "Sorry, we don't get a lot of women in fancy dresses hanging out in the engineering lounge."

Mia laughed, but it was awkward and after the man and woman got coffee they were out of there pretty quick. Leaving her alone, feeling foolish and even more out of place.

She looked up at those headlines, all those pictures of Jack smiling, looking worn-out but satisfied.

Was he really going to give up all that to work the Rocky M?

She looked sideways at her reflection in the stainless-steel fridge.

He's going to give up all that for me? she wondered. She didn't even come close to fitting into his world.

But it doesn't matter, she told herself, closing her eyes and turning away from the clippings. *It's a world Jack is leaving behind.*

But she was having more and more difficulty believing that.

Mia wasn't sure how long this meeting was going to take, so she kept her shoes on and sat down with her coffee and an ancient *People* magazine she found in the couch cushions, determined to keep her chin up.

More people came and went. Lots of men

in suits and she tried to be invisible and for the most part it seemed to work. But one crowd seemed to linger and she couldn't help but overhear their conversation.

They were talking about Jack.

"If he would accept the research position, we could keep him in the field for years at a time," one man said, taking a sip of coffee and then making a face before setting the cup down on the counter. "We just need to get to him before MIT does." He turned to a woman at his left. "And I heard Matt Damon was kicking around, hoping to talk to him about contract positions with NGOs."

Mia slumped down in the couch, her heart turning to lead.

The small group of people kept talking about Jack, discussing the possibilities they could offer him, but she tuned them out. Her head was buzzing.

She'd been right to doubt. Jack's world was going to come calling again. It was going to find him and he could only hide out on the Rocky M for so long.

So whether it was now or five years from now, Mia had no doubt that he'd leave. Again.

But he'd said he loved her, she reminded herself, carrying the words like a talisman.

Mia set aside her coffee cup, doubt like rocks weighing her down. And she waited. She waited long past when Jack said he would be done. The sun shifted across the sky, sending long shadows across the quad below.

She took off her shoes again.

Still she waited.

She crept back down the hallway. The conference room doors were shut, but she heard rumblings from inside. Male voices laughing.

Not a reckoning, then, she thought, her stomach slipping down to her feet. Mia looked down at her coffee-splattered dress, her bare feet covered in blisters and felt like a fool.

Hope, foolish and misguided, had led her far from where she belonged and it was time to go back.

She was an afterthought again.

Mia was done waiting.

JACK HURRIED across campus towards his condo, and even though he was only a few minutes away he dialed Mia's cell.

"I'm so sorry," he said when she answered. "I had no idea the meeting would go that long and then...when it was over, there were all these people, you are not going to believe what I've been offered—"

"It's okay," she said, and Jack paused as a bicycle whizzed across the bike path in front of him.

"There's no way it's okay," he said. "I've been gone eight hours."

"Just come to the condo," she said, the cool levelheadedness in her voice making the hair on the back of his neck stand up. "We need to talk."

Now he was really worried.

Five minutes later he was back at the condo and it was worse than he thought. The black dress was gone; instead, Mia wore a baggy long-sleeved T-shirt, the sexy heels replaced with cowboy boots.

Her duffel bag sat beside the couch, her denim jacket tossed over it.

"I'm sorry I'm late," he said, looking at all the signs of her immediate departure and feeling panicked.

"It's okay," she said, standing up from the couch.

"Clearly it's not," he said, pointing to her bag. "What's going on, Mia?"

"I think I'm going to end this now," she said, the shaking in her voice resonating through his chest. "Coming here was a mistake."

"What are you talking about?" he asked.

"Come on, Jack, it's been a disaster. You've been tense, I've been awkward."

Anger ignited in his chest. "Did you think it would be easy?" he asked. "This is the end of my career here—"

"No, of course not." She took a deep breath. "I just don't know how to help you. How to make it better."

"It's already better because you're here," he told her. "Mia, without you, I don't think I could have gotten through dinner last night, much less today."

She was shaking her head, his words falling on deaf ears. He wasn't blind to her awkwardness or to the tension between them, but those were caused by more than this trip. And he'd own up to his part of it, but she needed to do the same.

"You came up here believing the worst," he said, knowing it was true because he'd seen it a hundred times in her eyes, in the sad set to her mouth. "You never believed this would work. We were doomed from the start."

"I'm…" She bit her lip. "This is your world—"

"Not anymore. I quit."

"But there are twenty people here, right now, ready to offer you other jobs."

He blinked, taken aback. "How the hell did you know that?"

"I heard them in the lounge."

"Oh, come on, Mia, you're upset over something you overheard?"

"No, Jack. I'm upset because it's the truth. The ranch is my world. I belong there. I'm happy there."

"I'm happy there, too," he said quickly. Because he was. He truly was. He was happy with her. Wherever she was, that was home.

"Then what was the offer?" she asked. "The one you were excited about on the phone."

He licked his lips, feeling like a man being taken to the mat for something he didn't do. But if Mia was ready to give up on them, it only made him ready to fight harder.

"Water Summit is in Copenhagen this year. In two months," he said, fishing the pamphlet out of his pocket. "Oliver was going to be the keynote speaker and they've asked if I'd do it in his memory."

She looked at the pamphlet. "A week long?" she asked.

"Four days."

"And then…what? You'll come back?" She looked up at him, her eyes open wounds. She started to shake her head, denying him before he even had a chance.

"I want you to come with me," he said, quickly. "We'll go early, take a trip up to Edinburgh. I'll show you that castle. I'll show you everything you ever wanted to see."

He waited, his stomach in his throat, wishing, hoping and praying that the ballsy woman he loved would break through the fear and trust him. Really trust him.

Her silence killed him.

He grabbed her hands, crushing the pamphlet, but still she didn't look at him.

"I thought we were done being scared," he whispered.

"You're going to miss your old life," she cried. "It starts like this, a trip to Copenhagen, but soon you're going to wish you never said these things—"

"Never, Mia."

"No, let me finish. Your life…you should be able to go back to your life when you're ready."

"Listen to me," he said, gripping her head in his hands, wishing he could push the words through her thick skull and make her believe him.

"You saved my life."

"No, Jack, you would have been fine. You just needed rest and time."

"I'm not talking about after the bombing. I'm talking about when we were kids. You gave me something to be happy about. Something real. The rest of my life was crap and you gave me joy. Your faith in me made me believe I could do whatever I wanted. Without that…I don't even know who I would be, much less what I would have done with my life."

She was silent. Big, hot, wet tears fell onto his hands from her eyes. "And then…when you told me I needed to talk to my dad, sort out my past, it's like you did it again. You gave me a chance to reclaim some of what I'd always thought had been taken from me."

"I'm glad, Jack. I really am. But gratitude isn't enough to make our marriage work. We're from two different worlds."

He took a few deep breaths, his back against the wall. All these years, all the pain between them, the missed chances, and she was going to continue to rob them of a shot at real happiness.

"There is no 'my world,'" he said, tears building in his throat. "No 'my life.' It's *our* life. *Our* world. Maybe you're right, in a few years I might miss fieldwork, but you could come with me. See those places in your notebook."

She jerked away from him, but he held tight. He wasn't about to let her go. Wasn't about to give her the chance to run. Not anymore.

"But the ranch—"

"The ranch will always be there. It's our home. Ours."

She blinked as those words registered, and for a second Jack held his breath, waiting, hoping that she'd see it his way, but the silence continued and his heart dipped under a heavy weight of grief.

"Is this what our love is going to be like?" he asked, wanting it to be different, but committed to taking her any way he could get her. "I'll do whatever you need me to do to prove how much I want you in my life. I'll call the Water Summit organizers and tell them I can't do it, but will you ever believe me?"

FEAR SHOT THROUGH MIA like a bucket of cold water being dumped over her head. She shook at the sensation. Her head spun and she couldn't…she couldn't keep her emotions straight. Jack loved her. Was staying with her. So why was she sad?

What was worse? she wondered, her heart an empty vacuum.

Being left over and over again?

Or being left once and for all?

Was that the choice? A slow death from a thousand small wounds, or a quick one that was brutal and traumatic?

"I'm going to go call the organizers," he said, the fire in him banked. "Maybe it's just too soon to even talk about this."

He pressed a kiss to her forehead, long and sweet, and she wanted to die right there. In that kiss. Hold on to it, so nothing could get between her and that second of bliss. Of truth.

You're a coward, she told herself, hating herself for her fear. *And you're turning Jack into something he's not. Something tame.*

How long could he keep sublimating his wants to make her happy? How long would she like him if he did?

She heard him in the other room, shrugging out of his jacket. The bed squeaked slightly under his weight and she knew him so well she could tell what he was doing without looking at him.

She saw the curve of his neck, the resigned hang of his head.

But then the bed squeaked again and she heard him come back into the room. She spun to face him and her breath caught in her throat. Something hot pooled in her belly.

Jack was…different. Angry. His eyes sharp. His intent clear.

"This is bullshit," he said, stepping up to her. He searched her face and she felt naked under his scorching regard. "You're not this person, Mia."

She opened her mouth, but he kissed her. He kissed her so hard she fell backward onto the couch and he was right there, on top of her. Hot and heavy and perfect.

"You're not scared. You're the toughest girl I know and that's what I love about you," he said, pressing kisses along her jaw. Her neck.

"Love isn't going to turn me into something I'm not and fear isn't going to turn you into something you're not."

Bells went off in her head, the truth something she couldn't run from.

"I won't be brought to heel, Mia. Not because you're too scared to share my life."

"What are you going to do?" she breathed.

"Drag you kicking and screaming around the world. Show you everything you've ever wanted to see. I'm going to run that ranch with you. Give you babies—" He stopped for a second and her eyes burned with tears she saw reflected in his eyes.

Jack was crying. Her heart broke with love.

"Lots of them," he whispered.

The moment was too tender, too fragile, and he blinked away the tears, but she saw the truth. Had known it all along, even when she was too scared to believe it.

Jack loved her. Only her. And it was forever.

His hands slid up under her shirt, pushing aside her bra until he cupped her breasts in his hands.

He growled under his breath, up against her throat, the vibrations hitting all the right notes between her legs. "I love your breasts," he said. "I never said that because I wanted to respect you, but I'm done." He looked into her eyes, and she wanted to laugh at the desire in his face. He was a man transformed. Barely in control.

"You're done respecting me?" she asked.

He stretched his body out over hers. "Yep," he said, "no more pussyfooting around."

It took a moment, but joy and love broke through the fear, destroyed the doubt. This man in her arms, her husband, *her husband,* made her whole.

Laughter, healing and true, real and beautiful, bubbled out through the cracks in her fear, annihilating what was left of it.

He glanced up at her, wariness and hope all over his beloved face.

"Promise?" she whispered.

"That I love your breasts?" He palmed the heavy weight in his hands, teasing the nipples with his thumbs. "Yes."

"No, that thing about dragging me kicking and screaming around the world. About the ranch. About…about the babies."

He rested his head against her neck and she felt her heart grow, doubling and then tripling in size until he was enclosed. Never to be let out.

"I promise," he said, kissing the tears that leaked from her eyes.

"I'm sorry I was scared," she breathed, lifting her lips to kiss away his tears. They were the sweetest thing she'd ever tasted. "I'm sorry I doubted you."

He leaned up to look at her, his hair in wild disarray.

"You need a boss, Mia."

She smiled; she knew what he was really offering, what he was asking for—a partnership. Equality. "You think you're the man?"

"I know I am."

"You know what you need?"

He chuckled deep in his throat and arched his hips into her. She wiggled under him, delight soaring through her body.

"What you need more than that," she said, laughing.

"I need a wife," he said, looking into her heart. "I need you, Mia. I've always needed you."

"Couldn't have said it better myself."

* * * * *

LARGER-PRINT BOOKS!
GET 2 FREE LARGER-PRINT NOVELS PLUS
2 FREE GIFTS!

Harlequin

Super Romance

Exciting, emotional, unexpected!

YES! Please send me 2 FREE LARGER-PRINT Harlequin® Superromance® novels and my 2 FREE gifts (gifts are worth about $10). After receiving them, if I don't wish to receive any more books, I can return the shipping statement marked "cancel." If I don't cancel, I will receive 6 brand-new novels every month and be billed just $5.44 per book in the U.S. or $5.99 per book in Canada. That's a saving of at least 13% off the cover price! It's quite a bargain! Shipping and handling is just 50¢ per book in the U.S. or 75¢ per book in Canada.* I understand that accepting the 2 free books and gifts places me under no obligation to buy anything. I can always return a shipment and cancel at any time. Even if I never buy another book, the two free books and gifts are mine to keep forever.

139/339 HDN FC69

Name _____ (PLEASE PRINT)

Address _____ Apt. #

City _____ State/Prov. _____ Zip/Postal Code

Signature (if under 18, a parent or guardian must sign)

Mail to the **Reader Service:**
IN U.S.A.: P.O. Box 1867, Buffalo, NY 14240-1867
IN CANADA: P.O. Box 609, Fort Erie, Ontario L2A 5X3
Not valid for current subscribers to Harlequin Superromance Larger-Print books.

**Are you a current subscriber to Harlequin Superromance books and want to receive the larger-print edition?
Call 1-800-873-8635 today or visit www.ReaderService.com.**

* Terms and prices subject to change without notice. Prices do not include applicable taxes. Sales tax applicable in N.Y. Canadian residents will be charged applicable taxes. Offer not valid in Quebec. This offer is limited to one order per household. All orders subject to credit approval. Credit or debit balances in a customer's account(s) may be offset by any other outstanding balance owed by or to the customer. Please allow 4 to 6 weeks for delivery. Offer available while quantities last.

Your Privacy—The Reader Service is committed to protecting your privacy. Our Privacy Policy is available online at www.ReaderService.com or upon request from the Reader Service.

We make a portion of our mailing list available to reputable third parties that offer products we believe may interest you. If you prefer that we not exchange your name with third parties, or if you wish to clarify or modify your communication preferences, please visit us at www.ReaderService.com/consumerschoice or write to us at Reader Service Preference Service, P.O. Box 9062, Buffalo, NY 14269. Include your complete name and address.

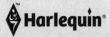